MORBID THOUGHTS

MORBID THOUGHTS

MICHAEL MCGOVERN

CARROWMORE.IE

Carrowmore Publishing
50 City Quay
Dublin 2
www.carrowmore.ie
info@carrowmore.ie

Follow the author at:

michaelmcgovernblog.com
facebook.com/michaelmcgovernwriting
twitter.com/mikeymcgovern
instagram.com/miholik

For myself.

CHAPTER ONE

I die a thousand times a day. You might think that's an exaggeration, but it's not. Every day I find new and interesting ways for my fantasy self to die in the confines of my own mind, and every time that I die, I feel a little less alive. Sometimes it's as simple as stepping in front of a bus. There is a soundtrack of shocked gasps from horrified rubbernecks as my body is crushed and flattened into a long, sticky tire-track of human flesh. At other times I imagine that a homicidal maniac bursts into my place of work with an 'Allahu Akbar!' and sprays me with bullets, punching holes from head to navel with my blood still dripping off the walls long after I'm dead. People would long after make claims that they were there the day Aaron Walsh died. Old ladies would read about it in their morning newspapers and tut at how far society had fallen since they last could chew a steak.

Sometimes I like to take the fantasy further and fast forward to the faces of my family when they hear the news of my death. How much would it hurt them? How much would they care? I think of all the things that would be said at my funeral and how quickly it would take people to move on and forget about me. I do this because death is a far more interesting proposition than life. In life, every morning is just like the last. I wake up and I wonder why the fuck I even bothered. In life, death is really the only thing worth talking about, because the thought of another day is simply unbearable.

It is fortunate that life does eventually end. We are all of us marching towards the reaper and his swinging scythe, but the vast majority of us are doing it the dull way. We are killing ourselves off with the silent disease they call routine. It fucking kills me – literally. I can feel my heart slowing at the mere thought of it. The thought that when I open my eyes I am going to do the same crap as yesterday, and I will continue to do it again and again until I can't do it anymore because I am shitting into a diaper for the second time in my life. Almost makes me want to do the noble thing and hang myself. There is no meaning to this mess, only expiration. We are no better than a carton of milk in that way.

Yet people keep searching for that deeper meaning in vain. There is no meaning to be found in the scriptures. They are the lies and fabrications of men too scared of the unknown. There is no meaning to be found at the bottom of a bottle either, just the sweet taste of oblivion flirting with your tongue. I'm sorry to tell you this, but there is no meaning in anything. It is all an accumulation of useless experience that the maggots add to their calorie count.

'So, what does one do when they come to the conclusion that nothing has meaning but they are too chicken shit to kill themselves?' I hear you ask. You do what everyone else does and pretend that there is something worth getting up for. That just around the corner there is an experience worth putting yourself through all this for. You think that you can't possibly kill yourself when there are so many experiences you haven't accumulated yet. You have to sky dive. You have to climb a mountain. You have to fuck a goat. Validation might be waiting for you just around the corner if only you would fuck that goat. These are the patches that keep the rusty boat above water, but even the most patched-up boat eventually sinks and gives in to the rust. We are all sinking without meaning and drowning in oceans of confusion.

I sit up in my bed and contemplate getting dressed. Yes, at the end of that rambling rant, I'm just as weak as all of you. Showering, brushing teeth, taking a piss, eating breakfast, getting the bus, going to work, coming home, eating dinner, watching TV, taking another piss and going back to bed. This is the day that is front of me. Sound familiar? No matter what your mother told you, we're not snowflakes. Some details vary, but we all, at some point, must take a shit and sit wondering if we remembered to buy toilet roll.

I need my small comforts to ease me into the day. An early morning wank usually does the trick. Nothing quite like a firm and steady grip on your manhood to remind you of the good things in life. Can't tell you the last time an actual woman felt compelled to grip it for me. Well, actually I can, because I don't even have to raise a finger to indicate the number.

Still carrying myself at half mast from my morning wood, it doesn't take much of a prompt to get myself to full salute. Fast and eager for climax is my approach on this particular morning. Who gives a fuck about the journey, I just want to get to the destination. Ladies and gentlemen, now arriving at Dublin airport is a big wad of cum, preserved magnificently upon a Kleenex for your viewing pleasure. See how it shines like a pearl.

With the first necessity of the day complete, I pick myself up out of bed and stare into the standing mirror. If the ladies could see this they would be screaming my name and begging for a piece. The name is Aaron Walsh by the way, if any of you ladies feel the need to scream it as I proceed with this tale of horror. You may not like me by the end of it, but that doesn't mean we can't have some fun along the way, right? I am taking the time to narrate this bitch after all.

Now, here is where I destroy those fantasies of you throwing yourself at me by describing the reality of what I see and my social circumstances. Well, for starters, I can't see shit without my glasses so let's put those on that mental image of yours. Are you feeling the love yet? If you are thinking hideous monstrosities that make my eyes look far bigger than they actually are then you are not too far off – stick with that image!

The eyes that are magnified so much; they're blue. They're kind of an icy-cold blue and rather dull. Definitely not that Photoshopped, film-star blue that resembles a sparkling oasis. More the 'Oh fuck, I feel sad!' kind of blue. It adds to that miserable-looking thing that medical books call a face. Pale and puffy, this isn't a face that you want to kiss, and don't go expecting smiles from it either. It'd only scare the children. My hair is something that you could cook chips on. Just a black, greasy mass that obeys no master. As for height and frame, they are both woefully average. I have some love handles, but who doesn't enjoy a deep fried mars bar every now and then?

Still think you could fuck me? Did I tell you that I live with my mum and my sister and I'm twenty-nine years old? How about now – wanna fuck? Thought so. You're not alone in that judgement. There will be no marriage, kids or white picket fences in my future, but what sane person wants all that mundanity anyway? When it comes to ladies and queers I'm a strictly no-fly zone. Probably doesn't help that I creep the shit out of anyone I come in contact with. Yup, I'm one of those heebie-jeebies guys. Everybody knows at least one. I'll hold that eye contact a little too long, I'll sniff your hair when you're not looking, and I'd probably parade around in your underwear if given the chance.

As for my circumstances, I'm not exactly happy with where my life is going, so don't judge me too harshly. It's not like I'm the first guy forced to live with his mother as an adult. Bitch still makes me a packed lunch though, so there is that.

Another erection. It's the gift that keeps on giving. Is it fucked up that I was telling you about my mother when that happened? Freud would have a field day with that one. I guess I could squeeze out another one for the road.

Let's see; need a mental image. Jennifer Lawrence naked as the day she was born, thighs spread and begging me to take her right then and there. Yeah, I think that should do it. Although it probably won't be the image that I finish on. Dozens of faces will flash past my imagination before the lucky winner gets the big finish. It's a rolodex of sexy faces and hot bodies and, just like flying in Peter Pan, all you have to do is think happy thoughts.

Again I go with the fast and eager method. I'm all about results. It always seems to take longer on a second pass, but is often twice as nice for the effort. I lean against the computer table and start masturbating vigorously, but my hand starts cramping up, not yet fully recovered from the first ejaculation. You'd think that doing this every day since puberty would give me the hand and forearm muscles of an Olympian weight lifter but no, here I am fighting through, like always. Maybe if I changed hands it would help. I leave poor old lefty on the bench enough as it is. I give it a try, but switching hands is like cheating on your wife with her sister while she's watching; it just doesn't feel right. I switch back to my right, which is still cramping, but I'm a masturbation warrior, damn it. There is a knock on the door. Perfect, just perfect.

'I'm fucking busy!' I shout, the perspiration on my brow a testament to that fact.

'Breakfast is ready!'

Yay, my mother talking to me while I'm stroking – that ought to help.

'I'll be down in a minute!'

She knocks again.

'What!?'

'You'll be late for work!'

'I said I'll be down in a minute!'

'Don't forget to put out the bins when you come home tonight.'

'Uh-huh …'

Almost there. Hopefully she shuts the fuck up by the time I squirt. I hear the sound of her footsteps moving away. There is a God.

'Oh Aaron, I need to take your dirty laundry for the wash.'

Shit! Did I lock that door? If not, her paying attention to that yellow 'DO NOT DISTURB' sign on the door is my only hope. Turns out it's not locked, and her attention has moved past signs to dirty laundry. Not enough time to tuck and hide. In fact, it's time to explode and stain another Kleenex right as she walks into the room.

'What are you doing?'

The only answer she gets is a sound in between someone having a satisfying cup of tea and a cow being violently raped. A sort of 'Mooahh!' if you will. Yes, I'm sure your cum noise is soooo much better.

'Oh my God! That's disgusting!' she gasps in horror.

What a drama queen. It's not like she's the first woman to ever walk in on her son masturbating. Granted, most of those mothers probably didn't get to see their twenty-nine-year-old son's O face up close, but you get the point.

'Haven't you heard of privacy!?'

'Um …'

She turns and leaves the laundry behind. I would bet that this incident was about to be locked away in the deepest, darkest vault of her mind, never to be brought up again. Some things are best forgotten for the sake of comfort when you live under the same roof.

As for me, it was not the ideal way to bust one's nut, but it's done now and there is no going back. I am as happy as I am going to get, despite some early morning embarrassment. It is much easier to cope with a dead fish than a stiff wooden log. With that thought in mind, my jeans slide on with ease. It hangs to the left in case you were wondering.

CHAPTER TWO

I come down the stairs to the smell of dead pig frying on a skillet. An animal was raised in a faraway place just to be murdered, strung upside down and drained of its blood. Its body was then chopped up into little pieces and loaded onto a truck to be proudly displayed on a supermarket fridge shelf. All of this so I can have breakfast without leaving the house. I hate people, but I do sometimes like the convenience that civilisation brings.

All of this organised murder is part of a traditional Irish breakfast. A sure sign that the Irish really do have a death wish; if the liver failure from alcoholism doesn't get you, the clogged arteries will. It also explains how my mother got to be such a fat cow. Oh yes, she's a fat one. You'd think that once you fail to see your toes past that mountain range you call tits and a belly you'd stop eating, but we all have our vices. Hers is just eating the farm, one animal at a time.

She started piling on the weight the day my father died. She ate the leftovers in the fridge when she heard the news. She ate every kind of takeout imaginable as she made the funeral arrangements, and then she cleared out the buffet table the day of. That was nearly eighteen years ago. Since then the plates of bacon have never been in short supply. A hippo wouldn't have been able to keep up with her. Not even a hungry, hungry one.

It wasn't always like this. She used to be attractive, until her features bloated out and aged. She was never in the Elvis Presley region of good looks, but the stunning transformation was very similar. If only she'd follow his fine example and snuff it while taking a shit. If it was good enough for the King then it's good enough for her. Perhaps then I could get the house for myself and toss my sister's broke ass out on the street. She looks like a street walker most of the time anyway, so she'd fit right in with the people who suck dick for heroin.

She's very similar to a slimmer, more attractive version of my mother. My sister Rachel must have liked the smell, because she was always full of her own shit. Ever see those people who look like they're about to hump their own reflection, pruning their face into a duck-lip pose while they take a selfie? That's her. She has hazel eyes that she got from my dead father. Brunette hair with a 'Please give me a sandwich!' body, pouty blowjob lips, and enough make up to make her the star attraction at the circus. She is the favourite these days. Like me, she's a school dropout, but unlike me, she is also unemployed. You would never hear my mother getting on her case like she gets on mine. At least I have a job! Rachel is always whispering in my mother's ear and giving her reassurances, you see. She finds my mother at her most vulnerable moments and swoops in like an opportunistic vulture over a fresh carcass of emotion. She finds her when she's crying about her weight, crying about her job, crying about the past, and crying about the future. At these moments, Rachel will say, 'It's okay, mum. Everything's okay,' and then they'll hug until my mother stops crying. My mother is a constant emotional wreck and Rachel is manipulative enough to feed off that. I have neither the will nor desire to put in the effort required to get those kind of brownie points. A mother's love is supposed to be unconditional, right?

There the two of them are, fat and thin; my blood. I know a lot of people have family issues, but it really is a sad state of affairs when people like this come from the same gene pool as me. I'm not without my faults, but at least I am self-aware and that gives me a leg up on most. Family is just an anchor of expectation that you can't possibly live up to. They live vicariously through you because ruining their own lives is not enough. Parents will give bad advice and claim it as wisdom just because they came first. Like that matters. Siblings are no better. They'll sabotage you the first chance they get, in some kind of jealous rage. Nothing hurts you like family. Nothing. The only reason for having one is for the satisfaction you get when you leave it behind, with the only reminder that they even exist being the voicemails on your phone asking why you never visit anymore. That is the dream. The only reason that I haven't left already is that it's too convenient not to. I sit and watch my money accumulate while I masturbate and play video games. It gives me an odd kind of satisfaction that cancels out my urge to leave. I don't know what I plan to do when I hit whatever the magic amount of money in my head is. The current idea is to go to Las Vegas where I'll buy a high-class hooker, along with some top-notch cocaine to snort off of her tits. I'm sure I could find an interesting circumstance to kill me before the money dries up. If I'm gonna go out then I might as well go out with a good story.

As I take my seat at the table, a puff of smoke assaults my senses. Rachel knows I hate people smoking where I eat. It's why she always makes sure she has a pack waiting. I hope the bitch gets cancer and has to talk through one of those voice boxes, forever sounding like a fast-food drive-through attendant. Would you like some fries with that cancer?

'Ever heard of electronic cigarettes?' I ask. 'I hear you can get them in cock flavour now. You should look into it.'

'Mum!' she protests through a cloud of nasal smoke.

'Aaron,' my mother warns.

I keep my mouth shut and offer Rachel a smug smile instead. You'd think an eighteen-year-old girl would have better hobbies than just smoking herself skinny and texting boys dumb enough to put up with her shit, but you'd be wrong.

While Rachel's smoke assaults my nostrils and puts me off my breakfast, Joe Dolan assaults my ears. My mother's favourite. You can tell a person's age by how good Joe Dolan sounds to them. Many times I have tried to introduce different bands and singers to her playlist, but she'll be a Joe girl until the day she dies. Good thing the man himself is dead these days, so I don't have to put up with any new material.

'The man's a fucking legend,' she often says.

'Fucking' is always added when you want to emphasise anything in this household. It's not enough to say the word alone. It has to be fucking this or fucking that if you want to get across how much you mean it. Joe Dolan was a big legend in her eyes, not a legend of the act of fucking, as the sentence would imply. Although Joe probably had his moments when he was alive, fucking tone deaf women just like my mother. In death I'm sure he would have been quite pleased when he reached the pearly gates to be informed by St. Peter that he had passed my mother's 'legend' test – an honour conferred only on himself and Charlie Haughey. One last notch in his crooner belt.

'You'd better be making a good go of this job of yours, Aaron,' says my mother, wagging a smoke-stained finger in my direction. My sister is nodding along with a self-righteousness that makes her look like an evangelical sermon attendee. Another unnecessary helping of dead pig is scraped from the pan onto the plate as my mother continues to press her point.

'There is no such thing as free in this house.'

'Yes, mum.'

'You're lucky that I tolerate you as much as I do.'

'Yes, mum.'

'Maybe if you actually helped around the house like a good son is supposed to.'

'Yes, mum.'

And on it goes. Once she builds herself up into a rant it's best to stand back and let that annoying wave wash over you. Tuning out gives me time to think about the important things, like whether or not I can lick my own elbow. Even if I was to give her proper responses she wouldn't hear them. They would just be a white noise background to the point she was making because what she says is always the most important thing to be said, don't you know?

'Are you listening to me, Aaron?'

Uh-oh, I lost track and held off the 'Yes, mum' a little too long. Time for a pre-prepared, generic answer that makes her feel her point has been acknowledged.

'I'll try harder, mum. I promise.'

'You fuckin' better!'

Mission accomplished. She goes back to cooking more dead pig that we won't eat and the incessant nagging stops for the short term. But there is always another wave just around the corner, as sure as the sun will rise.

I'm not that hungry and I've barely touched my plate. My idle stare falls upon my sister, who seems to take umbrage with my vacant gaze. Not many people can tolerate my gaze, vacant or not. I told you, I'm a hee-bie-jeebies guy.

'What the fuck are you looking at?' she barks.

'Something ugly,' I reply. Like with my mother, this is another automated response on my part. There is no wit behind it, just a reactionary statement. That doesn't stop my sister's face contorting like I've forced some sour milk down her throat.

'Mum!'

'Aaron!'

'Whatever.'

I'd rather stick my dick in a fan blade than spend any more 'quality time' with this anchor of a family. They always say that you should appreciate your family, since you only get one – but what are you supposed to do when your family doesn't appreciate you? I make the dramatic gesture of kicking my chair back and grabbing my coat.

'I'm off to work!'

I storm out, trying not to give anyone time to respond, but that almost never works.

'Don't forget the money you owe me!' my mother shouts at my back. She always has to get that last word in. A slam of the front door is the best I can do in way of response. This is going to be a long fucking day.

CHAPTER THREE

It's damp outside. Chances are that tomorrow will be damp again. In Dublin there are only ever two kinds of weather: damp and raining. If you chance upon the sun for five minutes in between, then you had best greet it with an umbrella just in case. Not that I'm complaining. If this skin ever saw sun I would peel, like a giant red banana.

I'm still in the process of waking up. My eyelids are heavy and the black rings underneath tell a story of one too many late nights on internet chat forums, debating who the best Batman was. Michael Keaton, of course. I don't know what the fuck 'Batboy69' was trying to achieve with his Christian Bale campaign. The guy from American Psycho, really? He sounded like he had throat cancer for most of the movie. After twenty-three pages of back-and-forth arguing, with my finger firmly on the refresh key, I'd like to think that I came out on top.

Fuck! There I go letting my mind wander again and I miss the fucking bus, along with another – and another. They're bastards like that. They're supposed to be spaced out so that there's one every fifteen minutes, but instead they conspire to buddy up and race past you all at once. In the time that it takes you to pull your head out of your ass you've missed forty-five minutes worth of busses in the space of three seconds. This is the glorious public transport system that I am at the mercy of on a daily basis. So much for being on time.

I lean myself against some stranger's garden railing and prepare for a long wait. Luckily, I have a whole playlist of music to help pass the time. I find with music that I usually spend more time searching for the perfect song to fit my mood rather than actually listening to anything. I get a good ten-second blast of everything in my library as my well-worn skip button passes them over, one by one. Eventually I settle for some Jack White and let my thoughts drift away with his screeching guitar. I much prefer music with a guitar that screams over everything. I always picture myself as the one on stage, and the instrument as my phallus, enlarging and slapping the face of everyone in the front row. It screeches and grows until eventually everyone gets beaten down by my massive guitar-cock. Even the merchandise lady at the back of the venue can't escape and is violently penetrated by the music. All of the ladies go home pregnant and nine months later they give birth to a thousand more guitar solos with my chords screeching out of their wide-open vaginas.

I'm not standing at the bus stop long before a cute little blonde comes along and goes to check the timetable. She has nice, tight features and probably isn't short of an admirer or two. I'm most definitely one of them. Here's an FYI for all you women out there: if someone of the male gender has ever looked at you, they've thought about fucking you. Even if your face looks like an inbred pug they've at least thought about it in passing, if only to say, 'Fuck no!' A man in my particular position can't afford to be so picky. I'll fuck a pug. As long as you score a three or higher then I could probably get it up for you. Probably. Give me a heavy girl and I'll use her fat creases to make a hot dog and provide my own mayonnaise. This girl standing in front of me is a solid seven, so it's only taken me seconds to visualise the variety of ways I want to use all of her holes. I take out my earphones and search for something to say.

'You just missed one. Three, actually,' I squeak in her direction. I wish that sounded more masculine. I hate my morning voice.

'Thanks,' she replies, almost as an afterthought.

'There should be one along soon enough.'

'Okay.'

Dead air falls between us, needing to be filled with something if the conversation is to continue.

'Shit weather we're having lately.'

Weather? The fucking weather!? No one under the age of fifty gets stimulated by a conversation about the weather, yet there I go talking about it. Predictably, she doesn't deem it fit for a response. Fucking weather.

'I'm Aaron. What's your name?'

She looks at me, but then quickly averts her eyes away from mine.

'Not interested.'

'No, I don't mean it like that. It's just, I thought we could have a chat while we wait.'

'Still not interested.'

She puts in her earphones, signalling an end to any discussion. Who the fuck does she think she is? I was just trying to be nice. I was going to maybe tell her how pretty she is. You see, this is why I'm still a virgin. Stuck up cunts who don't realise when a man is being nice to them.

I tap her on the shoulder. She doesn't pull out her earphones, she just faces forward ignoring me. She's probably hoping that I will go away. I shout to be heard over the music.

'I just wanted to say sorry! I think you are really –'

She snaps her earphones out and turns on me.

'Listen you patriarchal asshole! You're not entitled to my time, and I am entitled to just stand here and listen to my music if I want to, so why don't you just leave me alone and stop being such a creep!'

I hate lesbians. I congratulate myself on making a long wait even more frustrating and awkward as she goes back to her music. Funny how you can hurt somebody a lot by saying so little. She's such an inconsiderate bitch. We stand in silence for a good forty minutes, the blonde and I. She passes the time by texting people (probably about me), while I have little to do but supervise the crows and make sure they're not getting up to anything shifty. When too many get together, it's murder. Finally, after an agonising wait, salvation comes in the form of a chewing-gum bin on wheels: the number seven bus. It's a busy one, thanks to the longer wait. Already I can see that the top deck is completely full.

I let the solid number seven girl get onto the number seven bus in front of me because I'm all gentlemanly like that, if you hadn't guessed. It also gives me a prime view of her rear end. Her little skinny-jean ass wiggles in front of me as she pays her fare. At least I can still fuck her with my eyes. She moves aside and it becomes my turn to stare at the blank faced, soulless bus driver. I often imagine my appearance through the eyes of the bus driver. After years in the job, seeing face after face, it probably all blends into one blur of a person after a while. Chinese eyes, an afro, white skin, double-D boobs and a six-inch cock sheathed underneath some generic, unbranded clothing. To the bus driver everyone is equal, 'cause he doesn't give a shit.

I pay my fare and he prints my ticket without so much as eye contact thrown into the deal. I turn my head just in time to see the blonde take one of the last seats available. I look around and see that the only seat left is next to a decrepit old lady, whose skin looks like a chocolate bar that someone left sitting beside the radiator for too long. Perfect.

There is nothing fun about sitting next to the old. Not only are they a reminder that death exists (and is probably closer than you think) but they also smell funny, have weird habits, and think they are entitled to every-thing just because they've done the bare minimum of not dying. There is nothing wise about having near-triple digits in your age column. You come into this world awkward and unsure of yourself, you get a few years as an adult, where you think you have control of things, and then you go back to being awkward and unsure of yourself – only this time, you don't have your original hips anymore. If I were in charge, everyone would be taken out into their back yard at retirement to have a bullet put into the back of their skull. Imagine how much easier things would be if there was no such thing as this mysterious race of people called 'the elderly'.

I don't know exactly what it is about busses and old people, but they are always full of them, and they always seem to know each other. When they're not playing bingo or falling over in showers, they are on busses. I think the vast majority of them aren't even going anywhere. They just hobble on and chat to their eighty-seven-year-old friend Maggie, who also frequents the social hot-spot known as the bus. They do endless laps of the city, talking about nothing in particular. They'd probably love a conversa-tion about the weather.

If they don't take the bus for the social aspect, then it must be for the sole purpose of taking seats away from the young and the healthy. Even if you beat their zombie, zimmer-frame shuffle and win the seat fair and square, you're still expected to give it up for them. You just can't win – they're unstoppable. Seat denial is like a competitive sport for them. They don't even pay for it! They just sit there like the saggy bags of skin that they are, at the tax payers' expense. They make me fucking sick, doused in their over-powering perfumes to mask the stench of their slow decomposition. I bet this one in front of me, mashing her toothless gums into a jelly sweet, doesn't give a shit about me. She's happy sitting on her wrinkled, old ass with that smug look on her face. She's secretly enjoying this position she has put me in. She probably planned the whole thing. She woke up this morning knowing she was going to make some young stud sit next to her. It would be the highlight of her fucking day. Oh, I'm onto her and I'm not going to give her the satisfaction. I remain standing and keep to myself, but it's a useless exercise, because the old do like to meddle in the affairs of the young.

'Excuse me, young man. There's a seat beside me if you want it.'

I turn to face her big, toothless grin.

'I'm fine standing, but thank you so much for the offer.'

Bitch.

CHAPTER FOUR

Work. The last resort for those who don't find themselves being blown by groupies every night and cumming into the mouth of their childhood dream. My chosen place of misery and suffering is a computer repair store called 'Computer Heaven', probably named such because most of the 're-paired' machines up and die soon after leaving. We are kept afloat by our minimum charge policy that rewards our minimum effort.

It's a small place with a basic front of a counter, cash register, and various computer supplies hanging on the wall for the average walk-in customer. In the back is a bare-bones workshop space for all the broken machines that get left in.

The place is run by Frank Walters, a stern man in his fifties who has been around in the world of computer repairs for over two decades. He saved up his money and eventually bought this place, which he has been making a small but tidy profit on ever since – one over-charged repair at a time.

There are worse places out there and worse bosses to work for, but at the end of the day, it's still a job. It never fails to achieve groan status when I hear the morning alarm. The day was never supposed to start at 9am – that was definitely some Starbucks-sipping committee who put us on the clock, with a guy called Bruce eagerly laying the whole thing out in an elaborate PowerPoint presentation. Fucking Bruce.

Mr. Walters is waiting impatiently at the counter as I enter the store. You know that he has a bee in his bonnet when his arms are crossed like that. There are people who get upset about rational things like rape, earthquakes, murder and the like, and then there's Frank Walters, who will be on your ass for forgetting to refill the stapler. He is never majorly pissed – that just isn't his style. He just likes to have a good moan, ever since he passed into that annoying realm of 'old' on his fifty-fifth birthday. An age that I have determined should be the official bullet-in-the-back-of-the-head age. We could have a nice ceremony for it and everything. All of the family would come over with cake on Bullet Day, and then fight over your things once the deed was done.

Mr. Walters is a simple man with a lot of drive, or at least he used to have that drive. In recent years he's become complacent and let himself fall to that dreaded disease, 'routine'. Nowadays his life is his work and evening tea with his wife, Martha, who at sixty is even older than he is. Lord knows what she probably moans about. Most likely youths standing outside her front garden, acting suspicious as they kick their football about and laugh.

'You're late,' Frank Walters says with a short grunt of displeasure. People's urge to waste words on the obvious has always amazed me.

'Bus drivers – what can you do?' is my open ended response. It isn't washing this time, however, as he has heard me blame the busses one time too many.

'The day starts at nine, Aaron, and I am paying you to show up at nine. I suggest you catch an earlier bus, otherwise I will stop paying you for time missed.'

He says this as if he is expecting it to sink in, but what is a few minutes pay here and there to someone who lives at home and pays no bills? He continues regardless.

'Because of you we are already behind. Here I am working the counter when I should be in the back, working on repairs.'

Mr. Walters never raises his voice, even when angry. Probably because of that heart attack he had a few months back. He just lowers his glasses and gives you a look that puts you in mind of a disappointed father. Right at this moment he is looking down at me with those weathered, brown eyes. He is looking for some sign that his message has stuck, and that I appreciate the kind of disruption that I have caused.

'I'll try harder, Frank. I promise,' I say, lying to make the short term more bearable. Everyone seems to want that promise from me before they leave me alone. If they would just leave me alone without making me promise things, they would avoid a lot of disappointment.

'See that you do,' he says, seemingly satisfied.

'Get yourself settled and take over on the counter. I have a lot of work to get through and not an awful lot of time to do it. I'll be leaving a bit early to get to a doctor's appointment. Will you be okay closing up?'

'Sure, I guess.'

'I'd like to stay, but Martha is keeping on top of things and insisting that I go to this bloody appointment. I don't feel the slightest bit sick. These check-ups are nonsense really. You have one little heart attack and you never hear the end of it.'

And with that little external monologue concluded, he potters his way into the back to do some 'much needed work'.

I actually like it when I'm left to close up. It's the only time I am ever left to my own devices. If only I could shut the door on those pesky customers who always seem intent on spoiling a good quiet sit. Always wanting something, that lot. Frank doesn't pay me enough to deal with their shit.

I do help with repairs sometimes, but I am mainly the front face of the operation, dealing with customers who need somebody to shout at. There are a lot of those. People have their whole lives on computers these days, and if they come through the doors of a repair store they are already in a state of panic. Not that your average person needs much prodding to be an asshole to begin with. Money is power, and even small amounts of money can carry power. People walk into a place of business and act like they own the place because they mistake the power of their money for power owned, not borrowed. Take away their money and they are nothing. Insignificant whelps that dream of being something greater, but are too lacking in imagination. So they push, and they demand, and they stretch their meagre earnings as far as they will go, because it's the only real power they will ever know. They will die and the money will remain, only it will find a new pocket and a new ego to inflate beyond its worth.

For this reason, people who work in the service industry often have a lifeless, automated quality about them. Like they have agreed to switch off everything they are for forty hours a week, in exchange for a little money that gives them just as little power.

The worst thing about specifically working in a computer store is that people think you are a free advice service. Typing 'tits' into a Google search engine makes you an expert to these people. It's almost always stuff that your average six-year-old should be able to grasp, but somehow still eludes segments of society who are just too lazy to do the leg work. People will never try to figure out things for themselves if there is someone else out there who will figure it out for them. Heaven forbid they learn a new skill through the accidents of trial and error. One wonders how some people even tie their shoes in the morning without strangling themselves with the laces. It's always best to switch off when dealing with this and to think of that meagre amount of money and power you are owed. If only business could be conducted without actually having to interact with people. That would be some kind of utopia.

An angry customer marches towards the shop entrance. I brace myself for impact and get ready to give my usual spiel of pre-programmed bull-shit. You can always tell an angry customer by how they walk and how they carry themselves on approach. Their nose will be pointed upwards to the point where they are no longer being directed by sight and are honing in solely on rage-radar. Their stride will carry an air of entitlement with a little flushed redness in the face from when they rehearsed the forthcoming argument in the rear view mirror and made themselves angry. This guy storms in and shows his hand way too early, by shouting the moment he walks in the door. It lets me know what to expect and I adjust myself ac-cordingly.

'I demand to see the person in charge!'

The kid gloves and false, condescending politeness come out. This is one of my favourite tools to employ. If you speak in an overly polite manner you can often insult people without them realising they've been insulted.

'You can speak with me, sir.'

His eyes are black dots within narrow slits as he eyes me up, weighing in his head whether my face is one he wants to waste his breath shouting at. It is. It always is.

'I left my laptop in with you last week and you assured me that you removed every last virus. Yet when I started it up this morning, what do I see?'

'Viruses?'

'Viruses! Vile, disgusting viruses! The very same ones that I had before. What are we going to do about this, hm? How are you going to fix this!?'

'What would you like me to do?'

He chokes on oxygen as if this is the most preposterous question he has ever heard.

'Young man, I expect you to give me my money back and fix this problem free of charge!'

'We have a strict no-refund policy, but if you have the laptop with you now I will gladly take a look.'

'Really, I have never seen the like,' he begins as he puts the laptop in question on the table. 'In all my years I have never seen such terrible service. I'll be calling the radio. I'll be telling them all about this!'

I open up the laptop to see a barrage of pop-up advertisements on the screen. One advertisement shows a young woman riding a horse in a way that a horse is not supposed to be ridden.

'See!' he says with an odd air of satisfaction. 'You didn't fix it at all!'

I ignore the noise of his complaining and the spittle that lands on the counter in front of me with his every shouted word. It's only breath being wasted on a useless interaction. I go straight to his browser history instead.

'Ah, yes. Here's the problem,' I say, in the tone of a plumber who has just unclogged a sink.

'What? What is it!? Stupid boy!'

I crank up the sound and turn the laptop around so he can see. A black man with a massive tree trunk of a cock groans with pleasure as a midget works the shaft up and down with her tiny midget hands. The customer's face turns a pale white as the groans continue to get louder.

'You see, sir, we fix the problems that are there, but the one thing we can't fix are your browsing habits. Certain websites such as the one that this video comes from will continue to cause you problems. We were just too polite to point it out to you the first time.'

An old lady enters the store. The groaning intensifies. The man panics. I smile.

'Alright, alright, you've made your point! Shut the damn thing off!'

He slams the laptop shut, but the sounds of pleasure continue to play. His face turns red with embarrassment as he furiously flips the laptop over and rips the battery out, ending the sound for good. I can't help but rub salt into the wound with my false politeness.

'I assume that this resolves the matter?'

The man glares in my direction, but says nothing. He just takes his piece of shit laptop, nods awkwardly at the old lady, and leaves with his tail between his legs. There is a part of me that doubts if sex could ever feel this good. I turn to the old lady who is slowly recovering from the shock to her sensibilities.

'How can I help you?'

'I'd like to buy Google.'

'You'd like to buy … Google?'

'Yes. My grandson told me that I need it for the internet. Do you sell it here?'

And just like that my good cheer is gone. Is that bullet in the back of the head sounding like a good idea yet?

The rest of the day I am pretty much left unmolested by the masses. A couple of ink cartridge purchases and a dozen dumb questions that I do my best to answer without rolling my eyes. It seems like no time at all when the boss finally comes back out of the repair cave.

'She's all yours,' he says as he throws on his coat. 'Make sure to leave her like you found her.'

He walks out the front door and as soon as he is out of sight, the loud music goes on and the chair reclines as far as it will go. I begin to let myself relax as the heels of my shoes thud onto the shop counter. The only thing that comes close to beating going home is your boss going home.

'Excuse me!'

Shit. Another one. Her voice strains to be heard over the music. System of a Down sing about crying when angels deserve to die.

'Excuse me!'

'Yeah, yeah, just a second!'

I swivel in my chair and hit pause on the music. A damn shame. It was just about to get to the good part.

'What do you want?' I say as I turn, betraying a hint of annoyance that my time doing nothing has been rudely interrupted. The annoyance dies right there as I see who it is I'm addressing.

People like this do not exist in real life. If everyone looked like this, then Photoshop would be a thing of the past. She is the product of someone hacking the code of existence and producing a body with all of the most desirable traits a person could want. I have already seen a seven today, but what I am looking at now breaks the scale and redefines all the women that have come before. This woman turns that seven from earlier into a two. She is not even a pug now, more a Chihuahua that was disfigured in a bath of acid – and I don't fuck Chihuahuas that have been disfigured in a bath of acid.

Flame-haired, green-eyed, hard-bodied, with an ass like a speed bump. This woman is a fucking goddess, and she is standing right there in front of me acting like she doesn't know it. Acting as if looking upon her face is not an event to be documented. She looks me in the eyes. Her seductive green locks onto my ice-cold blue and I am at a loss for words. She doesn't break away or avert her gaze. No heebie-jeebies in sight.

'I'm here to pick up my computer,' she says in a voice like honey.

My mind drifts into fantasy. I lunge at her and rip her dress apart. I pull roughly at her bra until it pops free and her breasts fall majestically into my hands. I grope and I savage her entire naked body before I force her down onto the counter and fill her up like a petrol station pump. I fuck and I fuck until she can't take anymore, and then she says …

'Are you okay?'

Reality. There are no majestic breasts in this reality. There is a customer who shows only a glimmer of what could be, in her partly exposed bust. If only it were exposed a little more, then I could see areola. This woman was made to be fucked and swallow cock. Any other life pursuit would be a waste of that magnificent body. Some women are just not meant for the working world. Some women are meant to be chained and broken in half every day with passion and vigour. I realise that I have probably been sitting here silently as I take her in. She is starting to look at me strangely as she maintains eye contact. I really hope that she can't read thoughts. That would be most unfortunate.

'What's your name?' I finally ask. I put on the best professional face I can muster and try not to let her catch me undressing her with my eyes.

'It's Jane. Jane Flannery.'

'Let me just check in the back.'

I rise from my chair very carefully, taking a strategically placed clipboard with me to hide my massive erection. Once out of sight, I instantly fall back against the wall in an attempt to steady myself. My heart is thumping, wanting to burst right out of my chest and splat itself at her feet. It has been a long time since anything has even remotely raised my heart rate up from the normal. Who is this woman?

I wander over to the security monitors and stalk her through the camera. She waits patiently for my return. A woman such as this waiting on me. Something like that could go to a man's head if he wasn't careful. It doesn't take long to find her laptop on the shelf. According to the report that Mr. Walters made, the laptop is now perfectly fine and in working condition. I place my hand on it, but stop myself from picking it up. Right now she is waiting for me, and right now she wants something from me. That all changes if I hand her laptop over. I go back to being a nobody and she exits my life by the same door she entered it. She won't even remember me once she gets in her car. I would much prefer to be remembered. My hand comes away from the laptop and it stays where it is on the shelf. It is time for me to break the bad news to Jane.

'I'm afraid that your laptop is not ready for collection yet,' I tell her on my return.

She goes from serene to panicked in less than a second. It is nice to have this power over her. I wonder what else I can make her do.

'But I got a phone call saying it was ready.'

'It almost is. Just a couple more scans and such. He probably wasn't expecting you to get down here as quick as you did. It should be no more than, I don't know, couple of hours maybe.'

'Shit,' says Jane. I love hearing dirty words out of a pretty mouth. 'I needed it for tonight. I have a deadline and I need to get some stuff typed up. I don't know if I can make it back up here again.'

'Are you a journalist or something?'

'Something like that. More of a blogger actually, but it still helps to pay the bills.'

'What do you blog about?'

'Oh, I don't think it would be anything you'd be interested in.'

'Try me.'

'You know what, this is no big deal. I know of this internet cafe that opens late and I can probably finish my work there. I just really hate working in public spaces.'

Keep the urgency alive, Aaron. Keep her focus and need on you.

'I see from the files we have that you live in Sallynoggin. That's on my way home. If you want I can swing by and drop off your laptop when the last of the scans are finished.'

Her eyes light up. I did that. That was me. I am riding her emotions like a rollercoaster and loving every second of it.

'Are you sure? I mean, I don't want to put you to any trouble.'

'Oh, trust me. It's no trouble at all.'

CHAPTER FIVE

It is a lot of trouble. It is completely out of the way. I don't even drive. Yet something at the back of my head is pushing me on, telling me that good things will come from the deception. If following election coverage has taught me anything, it's that lying with a straight face is often key to success in life.

I flip the shop sign from open to closed and set her laptop down on the counter. If you have someone's laptop then you have a little, glowing, rectangle of a window into their life and soul. I take a couple of deep breaths and power it up. There is absolutely nothing wrong with it and it starts up as fast as a brand new machine. Mr. Walters has done a good job on this one.

I am greeted by a password screen and I consult the files to see what she listed when she checked the laptop in – 'Jane123'. I catch myself sighing in disappointment. She's lucky that she's pretty. I'm lucky she's easy.

I pound 'Jane123' on the keyboard and the password screen is replaced with a desktop background. It is a picture of her looking as lovely as I remember, but also a picture of a painfully average looking man with his arms wrapped around her. His stubbled smile is a mocking one. It says 'fuck you' with every bared tooth. He is of an okay build, but the slight belly paunch shows that he has never done a sit up in his life and that he is fond of the odd chocolate digestive. The hair on top of his puffy head is receding back at a rapid rate, and worst of all, he has those horrid ear gauge tunnels burrowed into the bottom of his ears. Big, wide, gaping holes stare at me from his drooping lobes. I don't know if it is just me, but I am of the strong opinion that if I can put my dick through your ear and rape the hole, then you have probably gone too far with your body modification fetish.

Every time I see a guy with a girl that is way out of his league I think about all the things they could possibly have that I don't. Is it money? A sense of humour? Maybe she used to be fat and thinks of herself as a little fat girl. She feels the jiggle of rolls that are no longer there every time he fucks her. In a way it gives me hope. Seeing his face makes her attainable. I'd gladly fuck the shit out of her inner fat girl, pounding her face into a trough of fried chicken while she squeals.

I smile at the thought as I get rid of Mr. Average and check out her music playlist. A lot of stuff that I'm not familiar with. Peaches, The Kills, Sia Furler. I hit shuffle play and I am greeted by someone called Amanda Palmer singing about how she doesn't want to be one half of an ampersand. Not really my style. Too whiney and self-indulgent. I can feel my non-existent vagina menstruating at the sound of it.

I go into her browser history, which is a treasure-trove of information. Lots of articles about female empowerment. She even writes for a feminist blog herself with such click bait article titles as '10 ways the media misrepresents women' and 'The trouble with rape culture'. I click on one of her blog posts and have a read.

All men carry the seed of violence within. We live in a patriarchal society that has been founded on their violence and oppression. When someone is raped all men are responsible, for they have perpetuated the culture where it is allowed to happen.

Women everywhere constantly have to look over their shoulders in fear of what goes on in the male mind. Fear of the thoughts they have behind that lingering gaze. There is no such thing as an innocent man.

This is around the time you will hear some men try to absolve themselves from their history and pipe up with a phrase like 'Not all men', like it waves away the injustices that we as women suffer on a daily basis. Well, in return, we say, 'Yes – all women.'

'Yes – all women' have been forced to tolerate unwanted advances because men don't know the meaning of the word 'no.' 'Yes – all women' have lied about having a boyfriend because a man respects another male figure more than he respects her. 'Yes – all women': because we are never 'just asking for it.'

I laugh as Mr. Average starts to make a whole lot more sense. He's probably the only man that willing to let her keep his balls in a jar. No wonder she was reluctant to talk about this crap when I asked her about it. All I ever hear from the opposite sex is crying and complaining. People in general keep inventing fictions to cover up their own incompetence in life. Men are the problem. White people are the problem. The government. Their poor upbringing. No one wants to take responsibility for their own mess. In her case it's clear that she has been too long without a real man. If she had a bonafide alpha thrusting between her thighs she wouldn't be writing such babbling nonsense.

I check her Facebook. I look through her pictures. She definitely knows how to have fun. Pictures of her at parties in various states of intoxication. Her at music festivals. Her on holiday. Her at the beach, wearing next to nothing. I linger on that one a moment.

She's a very popular girl. Her friends list is an extensive one. I wonder how many of these hundreds she really knows. Perhaps she is one of those people that 'friends' anyone she ever had a five-minute conversation with, or keeps track of everyone she ever went to school with – people best forgotten but now ever-present, thanks to the age of social media. Now you can know what people you don't give a shit about are having for lunch. If you're lucky they might even post a picture of it with a fancy filter.

She writes and illustrates books for children. The kind that usually have a life lesson at the end. She seems to be particularly well known for a series titled 'Debbie Danger', represented by a little ginger girl that is accompanied by her pet ginger tabby cat on the front covers. There's a whole series of them. *Debbie Danger and the Dreadful Dragons*, *Debbie Danger and the Devious Dormouse* and *Debbie Danger and the Dastardly Dog*. She definitely seems to be a fan of alliteration at the very least. An *Irish Independent* review describes the series as having 'the perfect role model for young girls in their formative years.'

I get bored of the surface stuff and probe deeper. I check her private messages. Most of it is your usual, mundane, run-of-the-mill shit, but I pause when I come across a conversation exchange with Jane and her best gal-pal, Susan.

Jane Flannery

I can't believe that fucking bastard!

Susan Keogh

whats he dun now?

Jane Flannery

He added her as a friend on facebook.

Susan Keogh

NO WAY!!

Jane Flannery

We've talked about this. He knows how I feel about her. It's bad enough that they used to fuck but now that they work together as well. I'm not going to be able to get the thought out of my head that it might happen again. He sees her all the time. He barely sees me at all.

Susan Keogh

im sorry hun. hope ur feelin okay x

Jane Flannery

I'm not sure how much more of this I can take.

Susan Keogh

u should talk to him again

Jane Flannery

Oh I will. Believe me.

I underestimated Mr. Average. It seems that he does have a set after all. It looks like the naughty boy is trying to go for a fuck down memory lane. He has only gone and fucked the door right open for me. I should send him a gift basket of lubed-up dildos that he can push through his ear holes, two at a time. I check out his previous squeeze by finding her on his friends list. The silly boy has gone back down to pug territory, obviously insecure about what to do with a woman from the top shelf.

I move away from Facebook and root through her folders and files in search of anything peculiar or interesting. It's the usual mess of stuff everyone has, mixed with useless things that should have been long deleted. That is until I come across a password protected folder titled 'Shhh'. The hairs rise on the back of my neck as I click on it.

I reckon the chances are slim but I give it a shot. I type in 'Jane123' and hit enter. The folder opens. I smile. She is so, so easy. There are a number of files, all of them videos. I click on the first one.

The camera is pointing up at the face of Mr. Average as he checks that it's on. He grins his 'fuck you' smile and his face is flush with excitement.

'Are you ready?' he asks, looking off camera.

'I'm always ready,' I hear Jane reply.

The world spins as Mr. Average searches for a good place to set the camera. He finds a spot with a good view of the bed, and for the first time I can see Jane. She is kneeling up on the bed, biting her bottom lip with a mischievous look in her eyes.

'What do you want me to do?' she asks, eyeing Mr. Average up and down.

'I want you to take it off. All of it.'

She begins to undress very, very slowly, each garment a tantalising tease as she drops it to the floor. Mr. Average circles the bed like a hungry animal, assessing how best to take his prey. The lace bra comes loose with a flourish, and her perky breasts fall and bounce into place. Her nipples are erect arrows pointing at her man, begging to be touched. Begging to be sucked. Her naked flesh is better than anything I imagined, but in this moment it is not for me. It is for Mr. Average, and Mr. Average can no longer contain himself. And who can blame him? He is merely average, at the end of the day.

He throws her down and rips the panties off her, exposing a wet opening that he wastes no time in filling, driving in to her gasps of pleasure. They start getting into it at the same time that I unzip my pants and also get into it. As he thrusts, I stroke. All the while I'm thinking, 'I could fuck her better than that'. I live in hope that sometime soon I will get that chance.

CHAPTER SIX

After a quick stop to the nearest book store, it's back to the horror of public transport. Only this time I'm not going home. I am going to her place. I am going to Jane's.

I pay my fare and sit on the top deck so as to avoid the decaying elderly, who are for obvious reasons averse to stairs. There are not many passengers upstairs. The ones that are there are my kind of people. They sit, eyes forward, reading their newspapers quietly or listening to their music at an acceptable volume. They are just looking to get to their destination as stress-free as possible. It is only when I walk towards the back that I notice the first undesirable.

There a heroin junkie sits, and I feel a shudder of revulsion at the sight of him. They are always instantly identifiable by the changes the drug brings to bear on their bodies. If you woke up tomorrow surrounded by heroin junkies shuffling towards you, you would think you were on the set of a George Romero zombie movie. The end of the world looks like a junky's face. Their eyes are vacant and their jaws hang agape, as if their rotted-out top and bottom teeth are reluctant to touch each other anymore. They are disgusted to even have to share the same mouth. Normally junkies travel in groups of two or more, scum associating with scum, walking around town like gutter-drowned pigeons, but this one sits alone. It's a fortunate thing since two will talk, and their volume setting is always at eleven as they shout their drawling gibberish to anyone who'll listen, about how the welfare wants to cut them off. They are the herpes of the city. Even his very presence makes me itch. I take a seat a couple of rows up from him and gladly turn my back.

Jane's laptop sits in my lap with all of its delicious contents. I made copies of course. Every video filed away for my own personal use. I even left her a surprise video of my own that will explain why her F key sticks a little.

Now, I know what you are thinking. You are thinking that I should stop right now and forget about whatever I am intending to do with this deception of mine. I've already pushed my luck, and if I have not broken some law, then I have at the very least violated a societal taboo. Perhaps that is so, but I did not opt into society and its structure. Chances are that you didn't either. It was already there when we were born and in my book (and this is my book) birth does not count as compliance. I have signed no contracts or agreements saying that I have to obey the rules that people I have never met set for me. When you boil everything down, it always comes to two forces that guide everything in life: the force of the things that I want to do, and the force of those who want to stop me doing them. Anything else is of minor relevance. The laws of society that you know and cherish do not apply to me, so you might as well disabuse yourself of that notion right now. It will go easier for you as you continue to read. There is indeed a small voice in my head that argues against my path, but it is very dim and strains to be heard. It sometimes tells me to stop and think of the consequences. You might have something in common with this voice, reader. I take that voice to a dark alley and strangle it. I pour gasoline on it and set that son of a bitch on fire. Then I wrap its remains in a weighted body bag and kick it into the ocean from a high cliff. I never have room for doubts. I never listen to that voice that tells me to stop. There are already enough voices outside of my head that try to tell me that, and I say fuck 'em all, and fuck you especially. I'll do what I want without the restraints, thank you very much.

I start to wonder if I could get away with discreetly sneaking another quick peek of Jane's naked flesh in motion while waiting for the bus to reach Sallynoggin. An irritating noise snaps me right out of that thought, however. It sounds like a swarm of bees, only much, much louder and obnoxious. Then the accents reach me, travelling up from the bottom deck, and my heart sinks. A horde of Spanish exchange students invade the bus. They invade all the way up to my deck, almost trampling each other in a lack of consideration for their fellow man. They shout down to their friends that are still on the bottom deck. They shout out the window to their friends that are still on the street. They shout to the friends that are standing right beside them. They shout, shout, shout, and make me wish for the junkie to speak just to drown them out. The Spanish invasion swarms Dublin in this way every summer. Human bollards that are always in the way of wherever you are trying to go.

There are not enough seats to accommodate them all, so I'm forced to scooch over and share with a Spanish teenager as her friends surround me from every angle with an annoying, hyper energy that frequently encroaches on my personal space. I can feel my ear drums cry out for mercy as the harsh Spanish tongue penetrates them. They come to learn English but they never have the courtesy to speak it. Even when they do, they speak it with a sound like someone scraping shit off their shoe. A constant, saliva-gargling 'sch, sch, sch' sound.

My head throbs and I try to think of something to take my mind away from the present. I look at their faces and think of all the things I can't do to them because of that force that would seek to stop me. I picture grabbing a handful of hair from the girl nearest to me and smashing her face as hard as I can into the seat in front. I imagine squaring up to the guy that is talking to her and putting my fist right through the front of his face and out the back of his head. I imagine everyone else screaming. Not talking in their shit-scraping tongue, just screaming like normal humans. Normal sounds. A scream sounds the same in every language.

'Sorry about this,' says a drawling voice, turned up to eleven. Even the Spanish turn around, baffled that there is a creature in existence that can speak over them. The horror on their monkey-faces is almost worth what I have to look at.

The junkie has his pants down around his ankles. The thing that he holds in his right hand? That's his flaccid cock. The thing in his left? That's a syringe, dripping with heroin. The junkie finds a juicy blue vein that is to his liking and pricks his prick. It is not a clean jab. Blood spurts from his cock like a peeing statue fountain. Soon both his hands and his junk are one big, red mess.

The Spanish start to scream, just like I imagined and speak urgently amongst themselves in the tongue of shit-scrape. The junkie is entirely unconcerned. He even looks serene. Absently he looks out the window and notices where he is.

'Me fuckin' stop!' he says as he reaches up to clumsily smear his blood all over the stop button. As he stands, he struggles to zip up his pants. He opts to instead just hold them up with his red right hand, still carrying the used syringe in his left.

'Wait!' he shouts, trying to get the bus driver's attention. The bus driver is not going anywhere. He is eager to have him off the bus and not his problem.

The junkie staggers as he walks, and falls towards the Spanish students with his needle point. They scream and scramble for the front of the deck. They are not even good enough to be human shields. They leave me with the junkie and the liquid hepatitis that now stains the seat. His pants have fallen and his cock drips into a gathering pool on the floor. He looks up and makes a glazed eye contact with me.

'Sorry mate,' he says. I hold his gaze and he is suddenly very sober. I speak to him, but my words are only for him. No one else hears them over the screaming Spanish.

'Go find a hole to die in before I put you in one myself.'

He opens his mouth to say something back, but thinks better of it, the words dying in his throat. He turns to action instead and finds his feet. He can't get away fast enough. He uses the hand rails for support to pull himself along the aisle, smearing his blood the entire length of the deck. Never a dull moment with Dublin Bus.

The Spanish don't come back after he is gone. They even stay uncharacteristically silent where they sit. I have a private, blood-soaked space all to myself for the rest of the journey. It is a relief when the bus finally arrives in Sallynoggin. It is time for happier things. It is time to go see Jane and let her know how I feel about her.

AN EXCERPT FROM
DEBBIE DANGER AND THE DASTARDLY DOG

Every day was special, but Debbie liked to think that this day was extra special. It was her birthday, and birthdays meant cake, and games, and presents, and all sorts of nice things.

Every year her parents would start the day by waking her up in the morning. Her mother would give her a kiss on the cheek and her father would give her a kiss on the forehead. They would say 'Happy Birthday' and let her know how much they loved her. She would give them kisses of her own.

They would tell her that her present was waiting down in the kitchen, just like it always was, every year. This part was the most exciting of all – for who didn't like presents on their special day? There was one thing that she wanted this year, more than anything in the whole world. She had wished for it on shooting stars, on pennies thrown into wells, on anything that a wish could possibly be made on. She dared to hope that maybe, just maybe, her wish might come true.

Eagerly, she ran down the stairs, taking them two at a time. As many as her little legs could manage. On the kitchen table there was a box. The box was baby-blue in colour and tied with a pretty pink ribbon, laced with gold. The box was very much expected as every year there was a box just like it, sitting on the kitchen table. The only thing that was different this year was that the box seemed to be alive.

It moved and rocked on the table, demanding to be opened by the birthday girl. Debbie's smile grew and touched her ears as she started to suspect that maybe her wish had been granted after all. Carefully, she untied the pink ribbon and removed the baby-blue lid.

'Meow.'

A ginger tabby kitten looked up at her with eyes as big as saucer plates. Debbie had been given her very own cat.

Butch, the family dog, trotted over on all fours to inspect this new creature, after hearing Debbie's squeal of delight. He cocked his head to one side, puzzled by what he saw inside the box.

'What is it?' he barked at Debbie.

'It's a cat,' she replied.

'Cat,' he repeated, testing the shape of the word on his tongue. 'Is a cat some kind of dog?'

'No, Butch. A cat is a cat and a dog is a dog.'

This confused Butch even more. What good was a pet if it wasn't a dog?

'Yes, it certainly doesn't look like any dog I have ever known,' Butch agreed. 'But does it play fetch?'

'No, it's a cat.'

'Does it do tricks?'

'No, it's a cat.'

'Does it guard the home against intruders? Wait, let me guess … It's a cat. What good is a cat if it can do none of these things? Send it back. You already have a perfectly good dog.'

'Cats do different things. Things that you can't do. You are both special in your own way and I love you both equally. There will be plenty of cuddles to go round.'

Debbie lifted the kitten out of the box and held it in front of her.

'I am going to call you Tabs.'

Tabs purred her approval and Debbie knelt down to give Butch a closer look at the newest member of the Danger family.

'This is Tabs, Butch. Give Tabs a kiss.'

Butch and Tabs did not kiss. Butch just growled and stomped away into the other room. The dog and the cat were not going to be friends.

CHAPTER SEVEN

Jane's house is a modest one. Not too big, not too small. It's sandwiched in between a pair of identical clone houses. Every house in the neighbourhood looks the exact same. Four front facing windows and pebble-dashed walls are the fashion of the day. It is as if the neighbourhood all got together over some tea and decided that it was a crime for houses to have personalities of their own. Wouldn't want them outshining their bland occupants now, would we? Inside, I imagine, they all have the same flat-packed IKEA furniture as each other. Their owners slave away all day to buy the same mass-manufactured crap that everyone else already has. It's yet another measure of meaningless life progress, along with the mortgage, car, and kids. Jane, at the very least, has a few flowers out front, where most of them don't. Daffodils mostly. They are the chocolate on a bland rice cake. My only concern is for what's inside. Everything else is wrapping paper to be torn away and forgotten about once the gift is in hand.

I nervously step up to the front door with her laptop gripped tightly in my sweaty hands. I ignore the hesitations of my racing heart and ring the doorbell. Almost instantly, a tiny dog runs to the door, yipping away angrily at this violation of its territory. The mutt mistakes itself for a German shepherd. I fucking hate yippers. They are more rat than dog and are constantly underfoot. Anything that can fit in a woman's handbag is not a dog. It's an accessory. It takes all my will power to stop myself stepping down on their fragile little spines whenever they are around. If I had a dog it would be a vicious, frothing thing. A true symbol of masculinity and worthy of the title 'man's best friend'. Not like this pathetic thing that barks at me uselessly.

I hear footsteps and the rat-thing scampers before its master. Her silhouette appears in the frosted glass of the door and then she is there. Jane Flannery, children's author, feminist blogger, amateur porn star, goddess. The flag is raised as I take her all in.

'You're a sweetheart. Thank you so much. You don't know how much this means to me,' she says as my mouth goes numb. I was fine on our previous encounter, but it just now occurs to me that I have seen this woman naked. It can never be unseen. Her clothing does little to disguise what my mind has memorised. Every freckle and line is visible to me as my x-ray vision works overtime on her fabulous form. I stand there awkwardly, not saying anything. I should have rehearsed something before knocking. Something smooth and sophisticated. I don't have anything prepared, so instead of speaking, I present her with the laptop as if it were some kind of offering to a pagan god. She takes it out of my reverent hands with a bemused look on her face.

'You really didn't have to go to all this trouble. Thanks again. I should give you a tip or something. Let me go get my purse.'

'That's not necessary,' I tell her with my heavy, sandpaper tongue. 'But if I could just use your bathroom that would be great. I've been holding it in the whole way here.'

She moves aside to grant me access to her home. As easy as that.

'Of course. It's up the stairs and to the right.'

I step across her threshold and creak my way up her stairs as she wanders into the kitchen to wait patiently for my return. I see the bathroom but I walk past it. I find the place where she sleeps instead. The place where she feels the safest. The bed is unmade, sheets tussled where she and Mr. Average have left their imprints. It is the same bed where they made their sex tape. I wonder if they fucked last night and sniff at the air for the scent of sex. It is disappointingly lacking and there are no used condoms in the bin by the door. My mind plays through the video from her laptop again, projecting it into the live space where it was filmed through the power of my imagination. I can see her pressed up against the wall as if she were really there, taking it hard, begging for more. 'Don't stop,' she says. When I reach out I can almost feel her there. It feels like my cock is the one she's taking. It is me that she doesn't want to stop. She wouldn't dream of it.

I lie in the bed next to her imprint and breathe in her smell, gently caressing the outline of her shape. I see her smiling beside me, reaching out to touch my face. She tells me that she loves me and we kiss. I almost lose myself to the fantasy, but I shake my head free of the illusion and Jane disappears back into her imprint. A man who is supposed to be using the bathroom has no time for fantasy. He must work to make his fantasy the reality.

I get up to leave, but my foot catches on something on the floor. It is the bra that she wore yesterday, and underneath I spy her panties. I squat down by the bed, raise them both up to my nose and sniff. Spots of blood stain the fabric. The coppery scent gives me a rush that I can feel pulsing through my veins. It is the scent that I've been looking for. My chest rises and falls methodically as I breathe it in and out, in and out.

As my eyes roll around in my head, they catch sight of something under the bed. A shoebox with something very peculiar peeking out of it. I stuff her stained panties into my pocket for later use and slide the box out from under the bed. A purple dildo of some girth stares at me. I don't even think, I just act. I take the dildo out of the box and bring it up to my mouth. I suck on it. I taste her dried juices and I cum. I cum while sucking on an imitation dick. I guess there's a first time for everything.

'Is everything okay up there!?'

Fuck! I let myself forget where I was. I take the dildo out of my mouth and throw it back in the box. I scramble as fast as I can out to the upstairs landing.

'I'm fine!' I shout down the stairs, the taste of her dildo still in my mouth. 'I … just drank a lot of water.'

'Okay. I'll be in the kitchen when you're ready.'

Too fucking close. I walk into the bathroom and give her toilet a quick flush before creaking back down the stairs and into her kitchen. She walks over with a twenty-euro note the moment I enter. I'm relieved to see that she doesn't appear to suspect a thing.

'For your trouble,' she says. I shake my head at the money.

'You've already paid. It's all part of the service. I could murder a cup of tea if you have some though.'

A slight hesitation crosses her beautiful face. This is more of an imposition on her time than she anticipated, but she raises no complaint as she sets the kettle to boil. Got to love Irish guest customs.

'It's a nice house you've got here,' I say in the guise of generic small talk. I don't really mean it. It's as bland on the inside as it was on the outside, but you have to start somewhere. At least I didn't say anything about the weather this time.

'Thanks. It's rented. I really wanted to save up and buy a starter home, but my boyfriend wanted to buy a car first instead. What he came home with was a little more extravagant than what I had in mind, so I'm having to wait a little longer. This place will do for the short term. Next time it will be my turn to decide the next life-altering purchase.'

'You're not married?'

'I don't really believe in that sort of thing.'

'Good for you. Too many people fall into that trap I find. Why chain yourself to another? They'll eventually just drag you down.'

'Oh, it's not like that at all. We both plan on spending the rest of our lives together. We just don't see why we need a marriage to make our love official. Weddings have always seemed tacky, vain and outdated to me.'

'Is that how you really feel?'

'What do you mean?'

'Just that you're not married and he'd rather buy a car than a house. Sounds like a man with only one foot in the pool to me.'

Jane smiles awkwardly and doesn't answer the question. The kettle clicks at an opportune moment and she makes two cups of tea, handing one to me. She invites me to take a seat at the kitchen table while we drink.

'What does your boyfriend do for a living?'

'He's an architect.'

'Very fancy. Is that what he's doing right now? He's out being an architect?'

She nods.

'He works very hard. He often works late into the night.'

'Either that or he's shagging a co-worker.'

She lowers her tea, a visible nerve hit. I fake laugh to try and put her at ease.

'Sorry, I watch far too many soap operas. My imagination gets away from me sometimes.'

'I'd rather not talk about my personal life with a stranger if that's okay with you.'

'Of course. It was very rude of me. I apologise.'

She clears her throat and changes the subject.

'Do you like working at Computer Heaven …'

'Aaron. It's Aaron. It's fine for right now, but it's not really what I want to do with my life.'

'And what is it that you want to do with your life?'

'I'm a writer at heart. I'm always working on stories in my spare time. I hope that someday I can get something published and have all of my work validated. Until then it is just a hobby that I enjoy.'

She perks up at this piece of common ground and seizes on it.

'Really? You know, I've actually been published myself.'

'I knew it! I thought that was you!'

She is startled by the sudden outburst of enthusiasm.

'Excuse me?'

'"Debbie Danger", right? I own the whole series. I wasn't certain it was you at first when you said your name but now I know. I'm a huge fan.'

I pull 'Debbie Danger and the Dastardly Dog' out of my coat pocket and place it on the table. This copy has only been off the store shelf for less than half an hour, but I have bent the spine and ruffled the pages to give it that well thumbed through appearance.

'You read children's books?' she asks.

'I used to read them to my little sister, but I think that I enjoyed them even more than she did. I wish there were more like you in the world, making wonderful stories for future generations to be moulded by.' I slide my copy of the book over to her. 'It's a little embarrassing, but I went home to grab this in case it really was you. Would you mind signing it for me?'

Her face is sceptical, but still she smiles, wanting to think the best of the situation. People will often chose to believe the unbelievable if it is the more comfortable of two options.

'Sure. It's the least I can do.'

She opens the cover and writes a short dedication on the first page before sliding it back.

'Thank you. I shall treasure it always,' I say as I put the book back in my coat pocket.

'You don't find the books too 'girly' for you then?'

'Not at all. I have to say that I really admire what you are trying to achieve. It's nice when you see someone fighting against the tide and giving young girls positive role models. It is long overdue.'

'It is refreshing to hear a man say that. Most of the time when the word feminism gets dropped it is greeted with suspicion from the manosphere. I often have to avoid talking about the topic in public as it can be met with hostility. That's why I like writing. No one can obscure your voice when it is right there on the page for all to see. If I fight with my ideas then maybe I can feel I am doing my part and not merely be a passenger in the movement. Be the change that you want to see in the world and all that jazz, right?'

'I actually consider myself to be a feminist, believe it or not. We are all together on this planet and I don't see any reason why we shouldn't get along and be equal. That starts with equal representation, like the books you're writing. Start them young and the change will come, I say. By any chance, have you heard of Amanda Palmer? I think that she is someone that you'd really like.'

Her tea clinks on the table as she puts it down suddenly.

'You like Amanda Palmer too?' she asks.

'I do. Why wouldn't I? She is a positive role model for women, just like we were talking about. You should look up some of her music. It's pretty powerful stuff. I particularly like the song "Ampersand".'

Her eyes narrow into suspicious slits. The unbelievable option is no longer comfortable.

'Aaron. Have you looked through my computer?'

I put on my best confused expression and attempt to play dumb.

'Of course. I do computer repairs.'

'Yes, I get that, but you've read my books despite them being aimed at young girls. You say that you are a writer, like me, and that you have pro-feminist views. You also just happen to like the music that I like. It all seems too much to be a coincidence. So, I'll ask you again. Have you looked through my computer?'

'We could just have a lot in common,' I suggest. Her cold silence answers that notion. I shrug and raise my hands into the air like an outlaw with a gun at his back.

'You got me. I guess it's time that I come clean. I haven't read any of your books. I don't know who the fuck Amanda Palmer is and your laptop was already fixed when you came into the store today.'

She opens her mouth to speak, closes it, then opens it again.

'I don't understand.'

'You would if you could see yourself with my eyes. When I first saw you I thought, "that's the most beautiful woman I've ever seen." I couldn't just let you walk out the door without some kind of plan for us to meet again. I had to find a way to get close to you. I figured that if I knew everything about you first that you might like me better, so yes, I did look through your laptop. But I did it to better know you and I hope that you can appreciate the trouble I went to so that I could impress you.'

She is gripping tightly at the table's edge now. Her lips are a thin, pursed line. Her words are careful.

'The book. Did you just buy that today?'

'On my way here.'

'Do you even live out in this direction?'

'Not even close.'

Her chair falls to the floor as she stands with a shaking fury, her outstretched arm pointing a finger to the door.

'Get out! Get the fuck out, now!'

I stand in front of her, pleading.

'No, no, no. This is not how this is supposed to go. Don't you understand why I did this? You are the one that I have been looking for, Jane. You are the person who can make this world a little more bearable for me. A man like me would worship a woman like you. Let your boyfriend go and fuck someone in his office. He was never right for you anyway, if he would ever think of doing such a thing. This time next month you'll just be complaining about him to Susan on Facebook again.'

The slap catches me hard across the face and staggers me. The second slap hits even harder.

'Get out! Get out! Get out!'

She tries for a third slap but this time I catch her wrist tightly in my hand and pull her in close.

'Let go of me, you creep!'

She starts to scream but I cut her off with a kiss. Her lips are like soft pillows, but they give me only the briefest moment of pleasure before her teeth sink in and make me recoil back in pain.

'You crazy fucking bitch!'

Jane scrambles to grab the sharpest kitchen knife she can find and holds it out in front of her in unsteady, trembling hands.

'I'll kill you if I have to,' she threatens. I can hear from her tone that she means it. I wipe the excess blood from my lip and spit the rest to the floor. Stupid fucking bitch.

'Don't worry, I was just leaving.'

She follows me out to the front door with the knife at my back the whole way. Little yipper snaps at my ankles as I walk. I step out onto the front porch and turn towards her one last time.

'By the way, "Jane123" is a shit fucking password for hiding your secret porn stash.'

She slams the door in my face and locks it from the inside.

CHAPTER EIGHT

That was stupid of me. She knows who I am. She knows where I work. Right at this moment there are probably a number of phone calls being made. Mr. Average will hear all about it, and, if she could get a hold of him, probably Frank Walters too – if not the police. It was really fucking stupid of me. By this time tomorrow I will be out of the job and probably much, much worse. Stupid, stupid, stupid! One cannot make excuses for this level of fuck up and still claim to be an intelligent person. Why was I so certain about things? Not really sure what came over me. I played all of my cards far too early and now it is going to cost me.

I get on the bus for the third time today. I am not in the mood for my surroundings as I head towards home. My mind barely even registers anything around me. It has fallen into the deepest well of thought, staring up at a troubled sky.

A giggle of teenage girls pull me out of that well as they board the bus. Some things have no respect for moods and demand attention, and a group of teenage girls is one of those things. They talk loudly about nothing of consequence and dress in a way that is inciting consequence. They try so hard to dress like the slut-whore celebrities in music videos, but they can't be more than fourteen. Their hips are non-existent. Their chests are flat. Their makeup unpractised and hideous. Their exposed navels and tight jean-shorts are sending out messages that their young minds are too immature to understand.

The aspiring sluts take up the back seats and continue to giggle about the boys who fancy them. Apparently Tracey let Derek feel her flat tit after school yesterday. When I think about what the future generations have to offer I often wonder would we not be better dropping the bomb right now and having it all over and done with. We are already on a downhill slope. Why not just drive off the cliff entirely?

One of the girls takes out her smartphone – named such because it has more processing power than she does. She starts to play some piece-of-shit boy band on loud speaker, thinking that the rest of the bus wants to hear her crap. They all start to sing along to something that barely qualifies as music with its over blown production and auto-tuning. I can't take it anymore. Who the fuck do these bitches think they are? This is my fucking bus! Mine!

'Turn that shit off!' I shout down the aisle. They respond with dislocated jaws of shock and crinkled pig-noses.

'You can't tell us what to do!' says the wannabe slut with the phone.

I laugh to myself and rise out of my seat, walking towards the back of the bus to face them. The other passengers are trying to look by not looking, because bus journeys are boring and they like scenes that they're not involved in.

I sit in front of the phone-holding, shit-spewing, über-cunt and look her straight in her vacant, nothing-happening eyes. I silently question why her parents didn't use contraception or at least use a coat hanger on her unborn foetus. She should never have amounted to more than a hasty pull-out dribble on her mother's thigh.

'No, I can't tell you what to do. If people could tell you what to do then your parents would have stopped you going out the front door dressed like a paedophile bicycle. Falling into a bucket of discount fake tan does not make you a woman. It makes you an orange pumpkin. Keep going down this life-path and eventually someone will rape you. Is that what you want, my little orange pumpkin? Do you want to be raped? Even if you consent to the first awkward boy that paws at your flat chest, you'll probably end up a dumbass, single teen mother raising another no-brain, orange shit much like yourself. So no, I'm not telling you what to do. Instead I'm going to tell you what I'm going to do. I'm going to take that phone and throw it out the fucking window. You can either turn that shit off or see if you can stop me. Your choice.'

The bus is silent. The music has stopped and no one speaks. All of the eyes are on me. The passengers are not even trying to pretend they are not looking anymore. Then it dawns on me. I actually said all of that out loud.

That was not in my head. That actually happened. What the fuck is wrong with me? I'm definitely slipping. One has to keep up appearances, Aaron. Fuck me was that satisfying though. I slump back into my chair and enjoy the peace and quiet I have earned. At least I'm not thinking about how I embarrassed myself in front of Jane anymore. I am thinking about how much I hate public transport. I really need to learn how to drive.

CHAPTER NINE

The last time I saw my mother and my sister Rachel, they were sat around the breakfast table. They sit in the same spot now, but the plate is set for dinner instead. A dinner that they are already eating and stuffing their pig faces with. It is like time has stood still in my absence. The food plate is the only clock in the house that has any relevance. I look at the plates and see slices of the driest roast beef imaginable. The beef is so dry that it has almost transcended into jerky status. In place beside the beef are rock-hard roast potatoes, watery mashed potatoes, burnt butternut squash and lots and lots of gravy. So much that it almost spills off the plate as an unnatural disaster, drowning imaginary towns with its flood of brown shit. Gravy is my mother's solution to every problem that may occur in the kitchen. Throw some of that out-of-a-packet crap on top and no one will ever notice how over- or under-cooked the food is. They will just taste that bland gravy giving it a sense of false moisture and be thankful it's there.

'You're late,' my mother says matter-of-factly, wasting words on the obvious. 'Did you put out the bins like I asked you to?'

'No.'

'Did you bring the money that you owe me?'

'No.'

'For fuck's sake, Aaron. One of these days you'll do just one thing that I ask you to do. Your dinner's getting cold. We started without you.'

'I noticed.'

'What you should be noticing is the time. If you paid more attention to the things going on around you then maybe you wouldn't keep being such a fucking burden to this house.'

Rachel snorts at the remark, but does not bother to take her eyes off her phone as she shovels some dry, gravy soaked beef into her bitch mouth. She doesn't see the cold look I throw in her direction. She would shudder if she did.

'What did you do today, Rachel?' I ask. 'I mean, besides sitting on your arse and trying to not get pregnant.'

She doesn't dignify the question with a response.

'You leave your sister alone,' says my mother as I take my dinner out of the microwave. 'At least she does the things that I tell her to do.'

'Can we not do this shit now? I've had a really rough day.'

'You've had a rough day?' she repeats in a sarcastic tone.

'You know what? I think I'll order a pizza and eat it in my room.'

'You'll do no such thing. You will sit with your family and eat the food I made for you or I'll plant you out in the garden.'

'Fine.'

I roll my eyes like a petulant teenager, but I do what she asks since that is what my family conditioning has taught me to do.

'Who is Rachel even texting anyway?' I ask. 'She spends her whole day looking at a glowing rectangle.'

'None of your business,' says Rachel.

I lean over and look at her phone screen.

'Who the fuck is Kevin?'

'Do you know what 'none of your business' means? Jesus!'

Rachel puts her phone on standby and places it away from her on the table.

'There. Are you happy?'

'Not really. Now we have to talk to each other. Your level of conversation hurts my brain.'

'Enough, you two!' my mother shouts. 'I swear, if we can get through just one dinner without bloody murder then I will die a happy woman. Aaron, how was work today?'

I put Jane out of my mind. She does not exist. I have not seen her naked. Her stained panties are not in my pocket. No woman matching that description walked into my life today. It was just another day, disappointing like all the others. I answer the mundane question like I would on any other day.

'It was okay. There was a jackass that wanted a refund, but I put him in his place by playing him a sample from his own porn collection.'

My mother almost chokes on a hunk of beef.

'Aaron!'

'What?'

'What is Mr. Walters going to think of such behaviour?'

'He hates giving refunds and I stopped one from happening. I'm sure it'll be fine.'

She sighs and shakes her head.

'I worry about you sometimes. Where is your life even going?'

I return her sigh and slouch back into my chair.

'Not this again.'

'Cathy at work was telling me all about her son. He enrolled in one of those back-to-education schemes. He wants to be an accountant. Would you not fancy doing something like that? You could get a nice, respectable job if you only tried.'

'I'm not going back to school.'

'It wouldn't be like school. It would be different. More adult.'

'I'm done with education. Sorry to be such a disappointment to you, but that's the way it is.'

'I'm trying to help you, Aaron, because it doesn't look like you are trying to help yourself. Can't you see that I'm worried about you?'

'Would you just leave it alone? I really don't want to hear this.'

I make a mountain out of my mashed potato as she snarls in my direction, incredulous that I don't want to hear about her concern.

'That's your problem, Aaron. You never want to listen. Start pretending to be a man and maybe you'll actually become one someday. You'll be out from under my roof and free to fuck up your life however you want. Until then you will listen to what I have to say. Do you think that Bill Gates made his money sitting on his arse? Do you think Mark Zuckerberg walked around with his head in the clouds? They were too busy making something of themselves, instead of living rent-free with their dinner handed up to them by their mothers. You should be taking notice of people like that and start turning your life around. Are you expecting to just sit up in your room for the rest of your life and let the world pass you by?'

I'm in this argument now, whether I want to be or not. I might as well engage.

'I hear this speech at least once a week and I'm sick of it. What about Rachel, huh? Where's the speech for her? You don't seem half as concerned about where her life is going. She's going out and fucking guys called Kevin on a nightly basis and you're not even a little bit interested. Do you even know who he is?'

'You leave Kevin out of this!' Rachel shouts.

'Or what? What the fuck are you going to do!?'

Rachel picks up her glass of water and throws it in my direction. I have just enough time to see it coming and dodge to the side. The glass smashes off the back wall of the kitchen and I rise out of my chair, towering over Rachel.

'Sit down!' my mother shouts.

'You see this shit!?'

'I said sit down!'

I clench my jaw and hold my tongue, but my eyes are daggers that pierce right through Rachel. She just smirks at me in return. That smug fucking bitch. I'd like nothing better than to wipe that look off of her face.

'You heard her,' she teases. It's like she's daring me.

'Sit down now, Aaron, or so help me God, I will smash a glass off your head myself!'

Reluctantly, I take a seat and focus on my breathing. I grip tightly onto my fork, putting all of my tension and pressure into it. My mother shoves an aggressive finger in my direction.

'Rachel is not twenty-nine years old. Rachel actually has a life outside of this house. You know where I see Rachel when she is twenty-nine years of age? I see her with a family. She is happily married and has given me a couple of grandkids.'

'You want that for me? The wife, the mortgage, the kids, the endless social climbing?'

'I want you to be better.'

'I am better. I'm too smart for all that shit. It's all one big trap people fall into and they don't realise it until it's too late. Sell that life somewhere else, because I'm not buying it. I see everything for what it is and I think, why even bother?'

She laughs in my face. Right in my fucking face. A piece of butternut squash is all that keeps me from grinding my teeth down into my gums.

'God love you. All this time I thought you were an ungrateful, lazy shit and it turns out that you are just too intelligent to do anything.'

Her continued laughter cuts me. She is not even close to being my intellectual equal, but still that laughter cuts me. I've had enough of this shit. Common sense tells me not to engage any further than I already have. The easy and familiar words of 'Yes, mum' are almost spoken, but I swallow those words down hard. This is not a day for easy words. This is a day where my mind escapes from my lips. Besides, this bitch has it coming.

'Shut up! Just shut the fuck up! You're so obsessed with where I'm going to be in a few years, but do you want to know where I see you? I see you in the fucking ground because you're a fat cunt who for years has done nothing but strive to be an even fatter cunt. You want to talk down to me? The last time I checked, you were stocking supermarket shelves for a living. So how about you shut the fuck up like I asked you to in the first place and let me eat this piece of shit meal that you made for me!'

The table falls silent. How about that for a laugh, you fat cow? My mother inhales deeply, and as she exhales she says each word of her next sentence as if the individual words were sentences in and of themselves.

'WHAT. DID. YOU. JUST. SAY?'

'He called you a fat cunt,' my sister volunteers, but my mother silences her with a death glare. She then turns that same glare back towards me.

'She's right,' I tell her. 'I called you a fat cunt.'

My mother rises from the table, and without saying a word, she walks upstairs. Rachel grins at me like she did when we were younger and I got in trouble. She is loving every second of the shit storm that she knows is about to hit. She would make herself some popcorn if only she had the time. I put my eyes on my plate and ignore her, forking some mashed potato into my mouth. Then I hear the thud of clothing hitting the bottom of the stairs. My mother marches back in and takes her seat, eating her food with a ferocity as she speaks.

'Those are your clothes at the end of the stairs, Aaron. I want them packed and ready to go by tomorrow morning.'

If this were a musical, Rachel would be on the table tap dancing in my face. She'd have all of her shit moved into my room by the end of the week, I'm sure.

'You'd throw out your only son?'

'I'd throw out an ungrateful little shit that doesn't know the value of anything. Do you even know how much the gas and electric bills cost? Do you know how long it takes me to do your laundry, or clean that room of yours that you refuse to clean yourself? You live here like a slob, rent-free, playing those dumb fucking video games all day and using my internet. Then you have the nerve to say what you just said to me. I've had enough. You think a girl is going to find you up there in your room? You don't know what life is because you don't have one. You're twenty-nine years old for fuck's sake! Start taking responsibility for yourself.'

My hand grips tightly around my fork, but it is no longer enough to ease my tension.

'I don't have anywhere to go,' I say through clenched teeth.

'Then I suggest you start looking. This is long past due. It is time for you to be a man for once in your goddamn life.'

It happens before I even know it is happening. My fork cuts the air as I ram it straight into my mother's eye. I hear a squish as I put a snarled pressure behind the stab, driving the prongs of the fork deep into the socket. Blood spurts all over my hand and there is screaming. Such loud screaming like I have never heard.

'Oh, shit!' I shout into the chaos of the moment.

I stand up and close my eyes tight, wishing for everything to rewind back ten seconds. Ten seconds is all I would need to fix this. But when I open my eyes there is no rewind, only slow motion. The fork still protrudes from my mother's eye and she is still screaming. My sister is screaming with her. I am screaming with both of them. Rachel makes a move to grab her phone and I instinctively backhand her to the floor from across the table. Her phone falls to my feet and I stomp my heel right through its fragile screen. A text message from Kevin disappears behind a spider web crack. Rachel whimpers on the floor, a bruise swelling up on her cheek.

'Everyone just shut the fuck up for a second and let me figure this out!'

My mother continues to scream, flapping her arms like a hysterical bird trying to take flight.

'I said shut up, you fat cunt!'

I grab the nearest sharp knife and thrust it right into my mother's throat. Blood sprays back against me as her screaming is replaced with a horrible gargling sound. Even the gargling eventually stops as the light slowly leaves her eyes.

'Fuck! Look what you made me do!'

The thought of murder had crossed my mind many times over the years, but I never thought that I'd actually do it. At least, not again. My mind races to a thousand locations as I think about all the potential places I could dump the body. This was too impulsive. Not smart at all. Murder needs planning and patience, not rash action. My mother is dead and the fantasy of her death has become the reality. She is dead and there is no way that she is ever coming back. It's time to start moving things forward. They will move forward whether I want them to or not and I need to move with them if I am going to survive this mess. I kill my desire for the past and root myself firmly in the present moment.

Rachel uses my temporary shock as an opportunity to run, but my shock doesn't last long enough for her to get away. She makes it as far as the hallway before I tackle her to the floor. She squirms underneath me, trying to break free, but I hold her still with my superior strength.

'Listen to me. It was an accident.'

Blinding pain clouds my thoughts as her knee finds my testicles. It buys her enough time to scramble out from under me.

'Bitch!' I shout at her back as she makes it to the bathroom and locks the door.

I slowly get back to my feet and regain my composure. I'm in no rush. She's trapped in there.

'I was going to try to make you understand, but now you're just being unreasonable. Open the door, Rachel.'

I get nothing but sobbing in response.

'Rachel, open the fucking door!'

I furiously kick at the door but it doesn't budge.

'Go away!' she shouts with a tear snot mouth.

'I'm going to kill you if you don't open up, you hear me? You're dead!'

I kick the door harder than the last time and I am rewarded with the satisfying sound of cracking wood. One more kick and the door gives way, swinging in violently.

Rachel is on me straight away with a can of deodorant and a cigarette lighter. She sprays the deodorant against the flame and I am blasted by the makeshift flame-thrower. I quickly turn my face away, but the arm I use to shield myself catches fire and the flames spread quickly, searing into my flesh.

I act quickly before she can spray me again, slapping the can right out of her desperate hands. With my flaming arm I seize her firmly by the throat. She kicks and claws, but she is powerless and completely at my mercy. I smash her head into the bathroom mirror. The shattered shards slice into her face, ripping holes that will never heal. She falls back into the bath tub, her blood spilling down the drain in fat drops. I jump right in after her as fast as I can, with the flames spreading across my body. I quickly turn on the shower and I grunt in a mixture of pain and relief as the water does its job. My arm sizzles and smokes as the last of it dies out.

'All I wanted was some fucking respect!' I shout down at my sister. 'Some peace and some quiet. You don't know the day I've had. I know you both planned this while I was out. You both wanted me gone. I should have killed you the day our parents brought you home, you fucking turncoat. I could have put a pillow over your head and smothered you then if I wanted to. Don't think that I didn't think about it.'

I go to pick her up but she is not quite done yet. A hard elbow smashes me across the temple and shatters my glasses. She makes one last attempt to run for her freedom, but it is her long hair that is her downfall in the end. I yank her back with a handful of it before she gets too far and I rip the shower curtain down around her head. I tighten my grip on the shower curtain until it is all she can breathe.

'Guess I get to smother you after all, little sister.'

She rasps and struggles against my efforts but her struggles grow weaker by the second until finally she does not struggle at all, her breathing at an end. My sister is dead. My whole family is dead. There is only me now.

A MOMENT FOR RACHEL WALSH

'I don't know about this,' I said as Claire dragged me by the wrist. My high heels click-clacked on the pavement as I tried to keep up with her eager pace.

'What is there to know? It's just a bunch of older guys hanging out. You'll love it.'

Claire had a way of getting the things she wanted, and what she wanted right then was for me to go with her to meet some boys that I had never met before.

'Aren't we a bit over dressed for just hanging out?'

If my skirt was any shorter it would have been a belt. I originally left my house wearing something else entirely, but Claire had told me to bring my slutty alter-ego clothes along. They were clothes that my mother didn't even know I owned. They were kept secret in a box under my bed and smuggled out of the house in the bottom of my handbag. I started the transformation behind the first secluded bush I could find. The heels, the belt skirt and cleavage exposing top all went on. I went into the bush as a plain caterpillar and when I emerged I was a painted butterfly.

'Hanging out is no excuse for dressing down. You look fine. I look amazing. It's all good.'

The house was a mess. Discarded beer cans from previous parties littered the floor. There was no telling how long they had been left there without a hand to pick them up. It was a game of hopscotch just trying to find a piece of stained carpet to place my next step. The smell of weed hit me the moment I stepped into the living room. There were a lot of guys there. They were smoking, playing video games and listening to music.

'Are we the only girls here?' I asked Claire, but she had already ditched me to go find a specific someone.

The guys in the living room appraised me with their eyes. I appraised them back, but there wasn't a looker in the bunch. I don't think any of them were under the age of twenty-seven either. Some were older than my brother.

'You can sit beside me if you want,' said the most eager of the appraisers. His eyes flicked up and down my body in a manner I found unsettling.

'No thanks. I'm just here for my friend.'

I hopscotched away from his flicking eyes and he failed to hide his disappointment. I found Claire talking to a guy that was much hotter than the others out in the kitchen. He was her real purpose for being there, I realised. I was just the piece of meat used to distract the slobbering dogs.

'I want to go,' I interrupted to tell her.

'Then go,' she hissed back in my direction. I was about to do just that when the hot guy spoke to me.

'Hey,' he said.

'Hey,' I replied.

'Kevin.'

'Rachel.'

It was instantaneous. I liked him. He liked me. It was one of those rare, perfect moments where life suddenly feels like a movie. I savoured the growing look of horror on Claire's face. She could see it too.

'I want to go,' she said after finding herself excluded from the conversation.

'Then go,' I said, struggling to keep a smile from my lips. This one time Claire would not get what she wanted. This was all Rachel.

Kevin was really hot, but he was also thirty. I didn't know if I was allowed to find someone that much older than me attractive. He asked for my number and I gave it to him. At the time I only gave it to him because I knew it would piss Claire off when I told her. I really didn't expect anything to come of it.

It didn't take long for him to start texting. The more we talked, the more I started to like him. We got serious pretty fast. He had a job and money and he bought me things. It was nice. The most important thing for me was that he didn't treat me like some idiot. He actually listened to the things that I had to say. He asked about my dreams. We lay in his bed while he rolled a cigarette from an Amber Leaf pouch.

'What do you want to be more than anything in the whole world?' he asked me.

'I don't know. I hear Aldi pay pretty well.'

'That's what you want to do more than anything in the whole world? Work for Aldi? Come on now, there are no limitations to this question. What do you really want to be?'

'Promise not to laugh?'

'I promise nothing.'

I hesitated as he licked at the rolling papers and made his cigarette whole.

'I want to sing. Sing like Rihanna.'

He raised an eyebrow in surprise.

'Are you any good?'

'I don't know. I've always been too nervous to sing in public.'

'Well that won't do now, will it? You'll never be Rihanna without an audience. The foot of the bed is your stage. I want you to stand there and sing to me.'

'I can't.'

'You can and you will.'

He held my gaze in silence. He stared until I finally broke.

'Alright! But don't you dare laugh.'

'I'm all ears.'

I shyly got up and moved to the foot of the bed. I remember that I couldn't look at him. I could look anywhere but at him. My face was a flushed shade of embarrassed red. I took a deep breath and I sang. He lit his cigarette and watched with his head propped up against a pillow. I sang with my eyes closed. I sang with all my heart, and when I finished there was silence. I couldn't bring myself to open my eyes again to see what he thought. I stood and I waited with my eyes held shut. I felt his lips pressed against mine. He put his hands on my hips and spun me around in a circle.

'That was amazing,' he said.

I opened my eyes and he smiled down at me. All things were possible with that smile.

I was going to tell the family about him, but you know; things happen. They probably already suspected something, since I never let myself get too far away from my phone. I don't know how they would have reacted to the age difference. Aaron probably would have just teased me and called me a slut. That's his usual way. Truth is, I never even slept with Kevin, or anyone else for that matter. People always assumed I was 'experienced' but the mere thought of sex always made me nervous. I would close up at the mere thought of it. Kevin was very understanding about everything. I did have other ways of keeping him satisfied. I think that helped with his understanding.

When Kevin first started texting he would only give me one 'x' at the end of each message. In his last message to me he gave me seven. I don't know if I loved him, but I think I might have. I don't know if he loved me, but I think he might have. I never loved anyone before and without the experience or time to figure things out, I guess that I will never really know what it was that I felt for him or how we would have ended up.

I wonder if he will get together with Claire now that I am gone. She always gets her way eventually.

CHAPTER TEN

It's no easy thing to drag a body. There is no life to give its weight support. No soul to make it comply. It is a dead thing that obeys nothing but gravity, and gravity likes being a pain on the back. But still I drag my sister from the bathroom, making slow but steady progress. I am silently thankful for all the years she spent throwing up food so she could live out her dreams as a walking rib cage. Once decomposition sets in she will be even closer to her goal. Minus the walking part of course. She's walking with Jesus now.

I drag her to the kitchen, where my mother still sits with the knife protruding out of her neck, and the fork out of her eye. She is a human cutlery holder. Her one good eye is wide open, staring at nothing, forever frozen in a state of shock and panic. It gives me the fucking creeps and that's saying something. I place my sister back in the chair where she sat before the incident for the authenticity of the moment. I even put her broken phone back on the table in front of her. Despite the obvious fact that everyone but me is dead, it is very much 'as you were'. I stand at the head of the table and address my family, as its only surviving member.

'Tensions have been running a little high lately, so I think that it's time we called a family meeting. That way we can get everything out in the open and sort some things out. Are there any objections?'

The table is predictably silent.

'Good. You are both now dead of course, so let me open by saying how deeply sorry I am for that. Things escalated very quickly and I lost control of the situation. The only thing that I will say in my defence is that I have been having a particularly bad day. I'm really not feeling myself at all, so I hope that you will not judge me too harshly. Do you think that we could find a way to move past this whole misunderstanding and start being a family again?'

I can see from the looks on their faces that they would like nothing more. They know they shouldn't have pushed me. A man can only take so much before he snaps, and I have taken oh so much.

'Thank you. I feel much better about this now. For a moment there, I felt terrible. This is some good progress that we are making already. I don't know why we don't do this kind of thing more often. It really does clear the air. I love you, mum. I love you, sis.'

I can feel their love radiate back towards me and I am warmed by it. Warmed by their cold, dead corpses.

'Since this apology thing is going well, I will do a couple more. Rachel, I am sorry that I smashed your phone. It kind of happened in the heat of the moment when I wasn't thinking straight. I know how much you like to keep on top of your social networking and the like, so if you are willing to wait, I will buy you a new phone for Christmas, and I will make sure to put it in the same hole I bury you in. I am also sorry for intruding on your bathroom privacy. You flamed me pretty good for that one.'

I turn on my heel and face my mother.

'I'm sorry that I called you a fat cunt. We both know that you are one, but I know that it is nothing you have control over. I know all about urges that can't be controlled. Ever since dad died you just haven't been the same woman. Which brings me to my next apology, and this one you might have a tougher time swallowing, but here goes.'

I take a deep breath as I prepare to drop the truth that I have been keeping secret for all these years.

'This isn't the first time that I've lost control.'

CHAPTER ELEVEN

You know what I hate? Flashbacks. Only assholes do flashbacks. There you are, enjoying the story and looking forward to seeing what happens next, and then some asshole says, 'Hey, let's rewind this thing to way-back-when to give you some context,' or some shit. Ruins the whole fucking thing. But if you haven't noticed by now, I'm just a little bit of an asshole. So let's give you some context about me – because I'm self-important like that. Don't worry, it is all going somewhere. This story does get good – or maybe bad, depending on your perspective. I am allowed to think the best of my bad. It is my story after all. My life. I've got a whole lot more sex and violence coming your way, dear reader. You're going to want to see what happens in this car crash, no matter how uncomfortable it might get. Have your seatbelt ready or else I'm likely to throw you through the fucking windshield.

My father, Jim Walsh, could only be described as a bear of a man. He was about as hairy as one, with the temperament to match. God help you if you ever disturbed the man while he was hibernating. His life was a boring three-way division of work, alcohol, and television. He was a 'jack of all trades, master of none' type who spent his days driving around in an unwashed white van with his name and phone number printed on the side. He would call over to the houses of little old ladies with more money than sense and 'tsk' at a wall they wanted knocked through or a roof they wanted tiled. It was always a 'tsk'. He would 'tsk' and say what a big job it was going to be, before charging them well over what they ought to have fairly paid. Then it would be home in the evenings for beers and dumbed-down American television that told him when to laugh. My mother would drop a plate of food on his lap and he would slap her on the ass and grunt by way of appreciation.

My mother had not yet become the fat, bloated frog of the modern day. At this point in time she was quite slender, with a body sustained by a chain-smoking habit that she passed onto my sister in the womb. She was a hardened woman of the workforce, even back then. She had come from a generation where it was more important to be earning money than finishing school. She had been working since she was fifteen and had seen every shit job that there was to offer. As a result she had developed such a hard, grizzled skin that the young, college-educated managers feared calling her out on anything. No fancy education or course had taught them how to deal with the fierce, working-class women of Dublin. She would wither them all with a glare and then take a smoke break with the other women of her ilk. They would bitch together about their incompetent bosses, and how unappreciated they were. Then she would bring it all home with her. It was a shopping list of complaints. Tom said this. Emma did that. My father would chew the food she gave him, eyes on the TV, throwing in the occasional 'Uh-huh' or 'M-hm' to give the impression that he was listening. I learnt that trick from him, in case you were wondering. Sometimes I think that my mother would have been just as satisfied if she had married a wall of brick and plaster as she was married to a man of flesh and blood. This was their life, day after day. Work, then home, dinner and TV, with a soundtrack of my mother's unanswered complaints.

In this environment I was given very little direct attention. Especially with my baby sister providing ample distraction with her shit-filled diapers. I was given free rein to shape myself and who I would become, as long as I was home by a reasonable hour and never brought trouble to our doorstep. To put it simply, I was a little shit. Childhood was a wonderful time for me. It was a time where I could be cruel without fear of repercussions. 'Boys will be boys', as the old phrase goes. Childhood is a time where you can be your true, human self before society gets a hold of you and forces you to abide by an unnatural set of morals and social conventions. Kids are free to destroy each other under the umbrella of their parents' wilful ignorance. Because of this, I would say that childhood was the only time I previously wore my inside on my outside. No one ever paid enough attention for me to hide it.

I didn't have friends as such, but I did have people that I dominated, and if there was one thing they respected in the Irish school system, it was dominance. My two primary victims were the unfortunately named Larry and

Barry. They had the misfortune of living close to me, so they had no chance to escape my constant schemes. They would often pretend that they were not home when I called round, but they always had to surface eventually, and when they did, they were mine.

As a child I grew a little faster than the other boys. They would have to wait until their teenage years to pass me, but back then I was physically intimidating to them all. I would push people around, trip them up, punch and kick them whenever I pleased. Larry and Barry got all of this and more.

In between physical attacks I would also undercut them psychologically. I would take great pleasure in twisting their heads around and playing them against each other. They were mine completely, whether they knew it or not. They were mine because I needed an audience to impress. An audience to notice how crazy and daring I was and spread the word around. An audience to notice my brilliance. I would make them tag along as I tested the boundaries in which I operated. Every day I would up the stakes, testing breaking points and discovering the level of shit people were willing to take from me.

I took to thieving pretty well. Larry and Barry would run interference while I grabbed whatever I wanted. It was never out of any need for any of the items I stole; I just liked taking them. I often would throw the items away after the deed was done and my fun was complete. It was a cheap thrill and its satisfaction diminished with every success. That only served to make me more daring. Eventually the day came when I dared to push things too far.

It may surprise you to know that I was a very avid church-goer. But I didn't go to find the Lord or cleanse myself of my sins. I went because I was bored and it was right there on my doorstep waiting to be fucked with. If I was to list why I do the things that I do, you would find boredom at the top of that list. I would go into the church during their off-peak hours and generally act like it was me and not God that owned the place. I would pass judgement on the old people who would wander in to confess or say their prayers. They were the practitioners of a dying faith with a dying faithful. I would speculate on their sins and why they needed the crutch of an invisible man to help them get over them. Their sins got wilder in my head with every imagining. So wild that my local town was a cesspit in the picture of my mind. I would play the role of judge and assign each of them a sentence in hell and imagine their flesh burning and flaking from the bone, their eyes melting until nothing was left but a blackened skeleton. Then they would be made whole and the process would start over again. They would burn continuously until not even their sanity remained. I had the power in this fantasy. Only I had the power to lessen their sentence and suffering. Their eternal souls were at my mercy and the thought of it would often bring a smile to my lips.

I would often bring Larry and Barry along and sit them in the confession booth when the priests were inattentive. I did this so that I could sit in judgement of them and own their souls as well as their time. Larry got a collective 252 years of fire over the course of my judgements, and Barry got an impressive 403. So impressive that I took to calling him Barbecue Barry, which he was not a fan of. His dislike of it only made it stick.

But like everything else, I would get bored of passing judgement, and boredom leads to other mischief. I would drink from the holy water as if in direct challenge for something to strike me down from above and prove its power. When nothing happened, I took it further and started to fill my Super Soaker with the sacred water. I would drown any sinners that had the temerity to pass by my garden wall. Sadly, no one burst into flames as a result. Just a lot of angry faces. Religion turned out to be a massive, boring disappointment overall, so I combined it with my other love of thieving to make it more interesting.

I started off small by stealing prayer candles without offering a donation, right under the watchful eyes of a Virgin Mary statue. I would tip the hot wax onto my hands and get little thrills of pleasure at the slight burning sensation. I would then get extra satisfaction by peeling the dried wax off of my skin. This was one of my favourite simple things to do as a child. I must have looked like quite the faithful Virgin Mary worshipper, covered in wax at her altar.

It was on one my most bored days that I noticed the padlock beneath the prayer candles. It had, of course, always been there, but it had taken a special kind of boredom for me to give it any attention. The kind of boredom that motivated me to do the things that I shouldn't be doing. The padlock was a flimsy thing. It guarded people's donations to the church, and it was flimsy because they lived under the assumption that no one would ever dare steal from a church. It would be like taking money from God's pocket. The thought was instantly enticing, because the very moment I thought of it I was no longer bored. My mind was full of plans and schemes. I was suddenly hyper-aware of every set of eyeballs gathered around me. The priests, the faithful, and even the statues themselves all seemed to be looking in my direction. This was something for another time, far away from the peak hours of evening mass.

I went home and stashed one of my dad's screwdrivers into my school bag. I smiled at the ceiling as I went to bed that night knowing what I was about to do. The very next morning I knocked for Larry and Barbecue Barry. I remember that their faces were particularly glum that morning. They always took it as a bad sign if I summoned them before school even started. I usually let them have as much as a walk to themselves at the very least. But not this day. This was a day when my audience was needed. We got as far as the end of the street with our school bags before I stopped them.

'We're going to be late for school,' said Barbecue Barry.

'Fuck school,' I said in response. 'I've got something more interesting to show you.'

I started to walk them towards the church and their feet dragged behind me.

'Why are we going there?' asked Larry.

'Why not?'

'I think we should go to school. I don't want to get into trouble.'

I pulled the screwdriver out of my bag and pointed it at Larry's throat, my eyes wide with a fierce determination.

'Really, Larry? Is that what you think?'

Barbecue Barry took a hesitant step backwards, unsure whether to run or play peacemaker. This was crazy even by my standards.

'I guess we can go to church real quick before school,' said Barry with a wavering voice. 'It will be quick, won't it, Aaron?'

'Yeah. Nice and quick,' I said with my hand steady on the screwdriver.

'Okay,' said Larry. 'Let's get this over with.'

I led them into the church. There were a few people there, but they were all forward-facing, with eyes on Jesus, hanging there uselessly for their sins. They had no thought for three kids who should have been going to school. I went straight to the donation box with my screwdriver in hand and threaded it through the gap in the padlock.

'What are you doing!?' said Larry in his best whispered shout. I ignored him and kept going.

Metal clanged against metal as I attempted to force the lock. It echoed in the cavernous hall, but the faithful were all too busy on their knees to take notice. Larry and Barry used my self-distraction to make a run for it before I could stop them.

'Fucking cowards,' I muttered as I tried again a little more forcefully. This time people did look in my direction, but the key to doing something wrong when in plain sight is to act like what you are doing is the most natural thing in the world. They looked at me kneeling at the foot of the Virgin Mary and just didn't put two and two together. Prayers were a far more pressing concern. It kept their minds dull and untroubled. The lock popped open on the third attempt with a satisfying clink. I reached in and scooped out the money box, claiming it as my own. I had done it. I had stolen money from God himself, but yet the achievement felt hollow. Larry and Barry had not stuck around to see my success. To really be worth my while someone would have to know that I did it. My eyes fell on the confession booth and my feet began to move towards it with the box of money still in my hands.

The confession booth had a warm and inviting darkness, with the pleasant musky smell of worn leather. This was where people came to cop out on being decent human beings. A few 'Hail Marys' and 'Our Fathers' and you could go back to your sinful ways for another week. The wooden slat slid across and in its absence I could see the silhouette of one of God's servants.

'In the name of the Father, the Son, and the Holy Spirit.'

I did the blessing with my hands as he said the words, but there was no meaning behind the movements.

'How long since your last confession?' asked the priest.

'Hard to say, Father. Probably the last time that my school forced me to do it.'

'What are your sins?'

'Where to start? I've said the word fuck at least a thousand times, but I think it is too good a word not to say. Fuck. It just rolls off the tongue. Fuck, fuck, fuck. What else? My baby sister has bruises from places I have hit her, but my parents don't know that those bruises are because of me. Oh, and I stole your money.'

'Excuse me, child?'

I gave the money box a shake so that he could hear it. I needed him to hear it.

'That right there. That's your money. I broke your padlock with a screwdriver and I took it.'

A brief silence hung in the darkness.

'I see. If you give it back now, that will be the end of it. We will forget it ever happened.'

'Give it back? Why would I do that? I just wanted you to know that I did it. My friends were too chicken shit to watch, but fuck them. Whoops, there's that word again. Are you going to absolve me of my sins now?'

'No.'

'I thought you had to. This is a confession box, isn't it?'

'To be absolved you have to want forgiveness. You want no such thing. You want recognition for what the devil has done with your idle hands. You should not take pride in such a thing.'

'Well, if you're not going to forgive me then what use are you? I'll be off then, Father.'

I left the confessional but the priest stepped out of his booth to cut me off, towering over me in his flowing black robes and white collar. His hand was outstretched for the money box and instinctively I pulled the screwdriver on him. His eyes went wide at the sight of it.

'My money now, Father.'

'This is a house of God.'

'And it's a very nice house. God's been living well. He won't mind me having a little.'

'I know who you are,' he said as I started to walk away.

'Have you confused me with the other kid you made suck your dick last night? Go on then. Take a good look and remember me well.'

I left the gobsmacked priest in my wake and stepped out into the sunshine. It was far too nice a day to be wasted on school. On that day I was my own teacher, giving myself an education. The lessons that you learn through your own experience are more important than any a classroom could ever teach you. I always learned what I wanted to know, not what people would have me know.

The money in the box jangled with every step I took. It was a satisfying but temporary thing. I did not steal the money to have money. They would eventually take it away from me if I tried to keep it anyway. I took the money to a bridge arching over a stream. It was a beautiful spot. Water trickled past as the sunshine danced on its reflective surface. If there was a God then this was surely his house more than any church could ever claim. I decided to give the money back to him after all.

I popped open the clasps on the box and peered inside, rifling through the notes and coins with my hand. They were meagre takings. Barely enough to pay for a few days of extravagant lunches in school. I sighed and tipped the contents into the stream. The notes fluttered and were carried away by the wind. The coins dropped with gravity and plopped into the water. I silently made a wish on each and every one.

On the trip home I heard a familiar engine noise roaring up behind me. I turned to see the dirty white van with 'Jim Walsh' printed on the side and my father behind the wheel. It was time to see where the consequences went. The van screeched to a halt as my red-faced father burst out in a fury to grab me by the scruff of the neck.

'Come here you little shit! Get in the fucking van, now!'

I was thrown like a human dart into the passenger's seat. My father got back behind the wheel and floored it towards our house. I could smell the alcohol on his breath as he shouted at me.

'You better still have that fucking money!'

'It's gone.'

'Fucking gone he says! Fucking gone! You'll be fucking gone before this day is out!'

Every other word was some variation of 'fuck' or 'fucking' now. It really was a good word.

'Get in the fucking house!' he said as we pulled into the driveway. The door slammed behind him as he shoved me into the kitchen.

'Think you're a big fucking man, do ya!? Let's see if you can take a punch like one!'

The fist connected before I even saw it. A low one, right to the gut. I vomited as all of the air was forced out of me at once. He had never hit me before. No matter what I did or how much I pissed him off, he had never hit me. Then came the second punch, and the third. My small, twelve-year-old body was lifted and thrown like a rag doll with every blow. He was very careful never to hit me in the face or anywhere that would leave a visible mark in public.

'Do you want to fucking die!?' he shouted as he took off his belt and lashed me with it again and again. He beat me with that leather belt until I was nothing but a crumpled ball of tears with hot welts rising on my back.

'If you ever. EVER. Do anything like that again, you will have breathed your last, so help me God! I will break your fucking neck with my own two hands! Now go to your room and fucking stay there!'

Every movement was agony. I had never taken a beating like it and as I dragged my beaten body up the stairs I decided that I would never take a beating like that ever again. There was very little sympathy from my mother when she got home from work. She even thought that I had gotten off lightly. She told me that I should thank God that my father didn't strangle me the moment he found me. He is a merciful one, that God.

I couldn't sleep that night. The pain was too much. I stared at the ceiling and thought horrible, nasty things about everyone I knew. My father, my mother, my baby sister in her crib, the priest, Larry, Barry. No one was safe from the evil within my thoughts.

I didn't stop thinking until my door opened the next morning. There my father stood, his third beer of the day already in hand. His face was pensive. He looked as if he had been thinking long and hard about something, but all he said was, 'You don't have to go to school today. I've already called in and told them that you have the flu.' And with that, he shut the door again. They were the last words he ever spoke to me. I sometimes wonder if things would have been different if he had said something else just then. An apology, or something with a little more affection in its tone. But he didn't.

I listened quietly to the noises of the house around me. My mother made breakfast. I told her I didn't want any when she asked. After breakfast was done, she left to go to work. That left only my baby sister and my father, who had no work lined up for the day. To keep busy, he had decided to give the front of the house a fresh coat of paint. I could hear the clank of his shifting ladder and the glide of his roller as he went about his business, only pausing now and then to get himself another beer. I hobbled into my parents' room to watch him work. As the morning wore on, the ladder clanked ever closer to the window, until eventually my father was painting everything around it. His paint-spattered overalls were suddenly in my direct view.

I winced with the pain as I forced myself over to the window. My father was completely oblivious to my presence. He did look down when I opened the window, but by then it was far too late. With a shove I made the ladder clank for the last time. He dropped two floors in two seconds and hit his head on the driveway with a satisfying splat. His head exploded like a dropped ketchup bottle on impact and the blood mixed with the white paint of an overturned can. With no one to hold the ladder in place and with the level of alcohol in his system, his death was later determined to be a death by misadventure. I was finally able to sleep.

CHAPTER TWELVE

'A father should never lay hands on his son,' I tell my family back in the present day, but they do not seem to agree with me. 'It sets a dangerous precedent. It was something that I could not allow to happen again.'

I can feel my mother's silence judging me. I imagine my shame to be so great that I can't even look at her straight and I act accordingly, but it is really just a pantomime. The true emotion is not there. I turn my back so that I don't have to look at her. Instead I lather a white dish towel with washing liquid and water from the sink. I pull up a seat in front of Rachel and start to dab away at the blood drying on her face. It has taken on the consistency of a thick syrup, and it takes a good, hard scrub to lift it from her skin. I have to hold her head firmly in place while I clean so that she does not slump lifelessly to the floor.

'I'm sorry, okay?' I say to my mother. 'I'm sorry that you had to raise us alone all these years. I'm sorry that your grief made you become a whale, but you have to believe me when I say that he had it coming. If he had a taste for beating me then he was going to do it again and again. I had no choice. Especially since you didn't raise one finger in objection. You could have tried to protect me, but you didn't. Where was my mother then? I was lucky that he didn't strangle me, you said.'

The white dish towel is now stained entirely red as I mop up the last of the blood on Rachel. The holes that have been cut into her face stretch and flap like many talking mouths as I scrub at the last stubborn spots. My mother stares at my back with her one wide eye. I imagine that she is waiting for the gravity of what I have done to sink in. I've had enough of this apology pantomime. I rise and turn to face her, with my finger wagging in righteous fury.

'You know what? Fuck you! Why do you get to judge me? Is it because you died? That was so fifteen minutes ago, get over it. How about I pass out a little judgement of my own? There's plenty to go 'round. How about how you never supported me like a mother is supposed to, or gave me anything resembling positive encouragement? You put all of your pressure and expectations on me just because you had to live a shit life when you were growing up. Well, guess what? I'm not you, thank fuck. You thought of me as some useless lump you could push around. You never gave me the benefit of the doubt. You were always undermining me, cutting my confidence out from under me. Nit picking at this, nit picking at that. No matter what I did, I was a failure and a fuck-up to you. Nothing ever good enough.'

She is the perfect audience in death. There are no interruptions or shouted counter-points, she just sits there, listening. I should have murdered her sooner, because this is a mother that I can get on board with. Perhaps I'll have her stuffed and placed in the corner of the room. That way I will never be without an audience again. A mother who is always attentive and lets me have the last word.

'You sit here and you talk about trivial bullshit like bills and cleaning. Do you think any of that matters now? In your present state I don't think you'll have to worry about any of that ever again. Your head has forever been clouded by the maintenance of the mundane and ordinary. You keep making the effort to preserve a shitty life that you don't even want. It seems that you want this for me too, but I'm better than that. I'm better than you. Yes, I'm smart. I'm a fucking genius, in fact – but people around here are too stuck up their own arses to notice, or give me any of the credit that I'm due. There has never been another like me. I am all there is.

'The reason I don't do the shit that you want me to do is that I'm too smart to fall into the trap of playing society's games. Do you really want to turn your special son into a clone of everyone else that came before? I'm not Mark Zuckerberg, and I'm not Bill Gates. I'm something else entirely. Something new.'

I bring the chair over to sit in front of my mother. I shake my head with a sigh as I look at the knife and fork sticking out of her like a pin cushion. This will not do at all. I take a steady grip of the knife that is lodged in her throat and I give it a quick, hard yank. It comes free with very little resistance, leaving a death-hole where the smooth flesh used to be.

'Life is all one big trap and no one sees it because they are too busy playing along. As soon as you are born they are already speculating, circling like vultures over your crib. Find him a good school and he'll have a head start in life, they say. So they find you that school, and the teachers start to teach you lessons about life. The key lessons are, "Sit down," and "Shut the fuck up." "You can be anything you want to be, little butterfly; now sit down with all the other butterflies and shut the fuck up." Once they have beaten those important lessons into you, they start to groom. "Have you thought about your future?" they ask. Of course not, I'm a fucking kid. "What do you want to be when you're older?" I don't know, a clown? "You better start preparing," they tell you. So you do. You stop going out, because you have to stay at home and prepare. All of your life is dependent on a piece of paper that says you are prepared. You do everything to get that piece of paper, because they tell you that you need it. You forget how to be a kid. You worry. You worry too much.

'You get that piece of paper, and they tell you that you have to make a decision. "Who are you going to be for the rest of your life?" You have a bad case of acne, you're a hopeless virgin, you can't even buy legal alcohol, and you're still trying to figure out what this "life" thing is, but you have to choose now, because everyone else had to. The biggest crime you could commit is daring to not be like them. So they tell you that the key to happiness is to walk in their shoes. They tell you this because misery loves company. But that is not me. Fuck doing what they expect. I will be miserable on my own terms.'

The fork in the eye is next. I go with same technique I used with the knife: I just reach up and pull. This time it doesn't go so smoothly. The fork comes out of the socket, but the eyeball comes with it. It stays skewered to the fork like a meatball, attached to the head only by a long and bloody string of spaghetti. I can't stop myself from laughing at the sheer absurdity of it. It is tempting to think of it as a little appetiser and pop it in my mouth for the sake of more laughs. I mean, it is already there on the fork and everything, but I suppress the urge. I may be a murderer, but I'm not a cannibal. That's for savages.

'Killing dad, now that was unexpected. That was a little something of the real me. Now that I have had time to digest what's happened here tonight, I don't think I'm sorry at all, actually. I felt that I should say something earlier when I told you, but that's part of the conditioning that I am trying to shake off. I've searched inside myself and there is nothing there for the man I used to call "father". I would have killed him some other way eventually, possibly here with you tonight. There isn't even any feeling inside of me for you or Rachel, even though I sit here right now talking to your cold, dead corpses. You are all nothing to me in the end. Family is just a footnote in my development. It is time for me to start accepting who I actually am. It looks like killing is a part of that. It's time that you met your real son. My name is Aaron Walsh, and I'm a killer.'

I take the fork out of my mother's eyeball and do the best I can to cram the stabbed orb back into its socket. It takes a good bit of fidgeting and rotating with my fingers before I can finally get it to sit somewhat right. She's a little bit cross-eyed, but it will serve for the purposes I have in mind.

'There. Good as new.'

With my mother and sister both presentable, I stand and address the table once more.

'It seems we have hit the point of no return and if my time is to come, it has to be now. I wanted you looking your best because I've decided that you both will meet a very special person in my life tonight. Her name is Jane, and I think you're going to love her.'

A MOMENT FOR MARY WALSH

'Aaron, wake up,' I said as I gently nudged my twelve-year-old son. He opened his eyes, but turned back into his pillow to better ignore me. I drew back the blinds to let some light into the room, but it was still pretty bleak outside, on account of the early hour.

'Come on, Aaron. I have to drop you off at your Aunt Joan's before I go to work.'

He squinted at the open window and pulled the covers over his head.

'It's not even bright out,' he mumbled.

'You still have to go.'

Snoring was his response to that notion.

'I said get up!'

I took hold of his bed covers and ripped them away, taking his source of comfort and exposing him to the early morning. He was not at all happy, but at least he was awake.

I strapped Rachel into her car seat and Aaron sat beside her with a sullen expression on his face. I tried making conversation once we were on the road, but he responded by pulling out his Gameboy and blocking out everything else around him. I was starting to worry about Aaron. He didn't seem at all affected by his father's recent death. He even looked bored at the funeral, if such a thing was possible. I needed to have a long talk with him, but it was becoming increasingly hard to find the time. Everything started to pile up the moment I became a single mother of two.

Aaron walked on ahead of me as I struggled with baby Rachel in my arms. Aaron's little cousin Tommy ran up to him with a chocolate-covered face as he entered the house.

'Hey, Aaron! Wanna play?' he said as he waved a Transformers action figure in Aaron's direction.

'Fuck off,' was Aaron's response.

'Aaron!' I shouted after him. He looked back at me and frowned. Then with a sigh he turned back to Tommy.

'Sure. Let's play. Whatever.'

The two of them disappeared into the living room together. I brought Rachel into the kitchen where Joan was sitting, having her first coffee of the morning.

'Thanks for doing this again, Joan. You're really helping me out,' I said as I got Rachel settled.

'Have a seat, Mary.'

'I can't stop. I'm going to be late for work.'

'Have a seat. We need to talk.'

I did not like the sound of that. I pulled out a chair and took a seat.

'I can't look after your kids anymore,' she said. Straight and to the point.

'What? Why?'

'I wanted to help you out when my brother died and I think that I have. But this arrangement can't continue.'

'Please, Joan. I really need this. I can't work and look after them at the same time. Just until I get back on my feet and then I'll sort something else out, I promise.'

Joan sighed and drummed her fingers on the table. Her lips were a thin line of contemplation.

'I didn't want to have to say this, but … It's Aaron.'

'What about Aaron?'

'He's a bad influence on Tommy.'

'What do you mean?'

'I think you know what I mean.'

'His father just died. He's having a tough time.'

'I don't want him in this house anymore, Mary.'

'He's your nephew.'

Joan stayed silent and avoided eye contact while taking a long sip of her coffee.

'I see.'

Joan had already made her decision and there was no use in arguing about it any further. Things hadn't worked out the way that I hoped, but I still had my pride.

'Can you at least watch them for today – or is that too much to ask of their aunt?'

'I'll watch them for today, but not any longer.'

'I have to go to work.'

I got up from the chair, but stopped myself at the door.

'He didn't leave me anything, you know. Not a single cent. Everything we had he gambled away behind my back. He gambled it away and pretended that everything was fine. Everything is not fine, Joan.'

'I'm sorry.'

'Fuck your sorry.'

I thought about my options as I got into the car. I was already working non-stop just to keep our heads above water. Aaron was going to have to stay at home and look after himself in the evenings. Rachel was a different story entirely, but childcare was another expense on top of the many that I couldn't afford. I would have to find another job and face a future where my children raised themselves. Never had I felt like such a failure before. It was strange to work so hard all the time, to always be on the verge of falling asleep, and still see everything turn to shit.

The tears came when I turned the key and 'Good looking woman' by Joe Dolan played through the car speakers. It was my wedding song. When I danced with Jim that night, the future was a happy place, full of possibility.

CHAPTER THIRTEEN

Looking fabulous is tough work, darlings. I know that it comes easy to some of you, and to you I say this: suck it. Whatever would Jane think of me if I showed up covered in blood and looking like I have been dragged through the rear cat-flap. A man has to look presentable if he is to win over the love of his life. Normally my idea of presentable is falling out of bed and putting on whatever clothes pass the sniff test, but this evening I have something more elegant in mind. Attire fit for a lady. Where to even begin? The blood, I suppose. Getting rid of blood is always a good start when courting a lady.

In the bathroom I strip and stand naked in a pool of my sister's blood. I turn on the shower to wash mine off and mix it with hers. The blood of family runs thickly together down the drain and disappears as if it never was. The burns she gave me to remember her by scream in protest at the use of hot water. This one will have to be a cold shower. My junk shrivels up at the prospect, a turtle retreating into its shell. The burns are actually not as bad as I initially thought they would be. Some pieces of my shirt have fused to the skin and that is where the pain is at its worst. I rip those pieces off now, taking the delicate flesh underneath away with them. I bite my lip and pound my fist against the wall with every agonising piece. I turn my oozing arm towards the shooting jets of ice-cold water in an attempt to soothe the pain. There will definitely be some scarring, but otherwise it looks like I got off lightly. I hear that chicks dig scars, so that's something, I guess. I'll make sure to leave out the part that I got them while murdering my sister. Saving orphans from a fire would probably play better.

I coat myself in some kiwi-scented body wash, and I smell so delicious that I almost want to take a bite out of myself. I then use some generic shampoo to take all of the long-accumulated oils out of my greasy head of hair. The instructions on the bottle tell me to 'Wash, rinse, repeat' but I stop after the second cycle. To follow those instructions literally would lead to a looping eternity of hair washing. It would be like getting stuck in a L'Oreal advert. 'Murder', the new shampoo by Aaron Walsh: because your death is worth it.

Once my uncomfortable, cold shower has concluded, I dry myself off thoroughly and my junk feels confident enough to emerge from its turtle-shell hiding place.

'Hey, big boy,' says my own voice from somewhere outside of me. It sounds weird to my ears, like hearing a recording of myself for the first time. I wonder where it came from.

I look down at the blood-tipped mirror shards that litter the sink and see the reflection of a dozen Aaron Walshes. They seem to move independently of my own movements – but it's hard to tell without my glasses.

'Put in your contacts, stupid,' one of the blurry mirror shards instructs.

I hate wearing those things. They give me a constant urge to scratch my own eyes out, but I obey the voice, as it sounds so much like me, and take them out of the cabinet. I place the contact lenses on my eyes and do the whole awkward blink routine until I feel them slide into place. The world snaps back into an itchy clarity.

'Now, what are we going to do about the rest of you?'

I follow the voice to its source, and it certainly came from one of the reflected Aaron Walshes. One of them winks at me and a second Aaron responds to the first.

'He needs to take care of those burns.'

I may be going crazy, but at least my crazy talks sense. I find the first aid kit and apply the ointment within it all over the burns' surface area. I then take a bandage and carefully wrap it around my arm.

'Are you kidding me? He's going to look like The Mummy when he's done,' one of the shards complains. 'Girls will fuck Dracula, and even those *Twilight* arseholes, but no one wants to fuck The Mummy.'

'Don't worry about it. He'll have clothes on. You can make anyone look sexy with the right clothes. Can we get some music in this hallucination?'

'Is that David Bowie?' I ask, but there is no need for them to respond. I can hear "Fashion" by David Bowie in my ear, clear as day. I can hear it because David Bowie is standing in my bath tub singing it to me. I decide that David Bowie singing in a bath tub is something that shouldn't be questioned. I just go with it.

I take the pile of clothes that my mother dumped at the end of the stairs and I put on a fashion show for an audience of Aarons and David Bowie. They all offer their critiques and opinions until we collectively decide that Sunday best is the way to go. I take my fanciest dress shirt and button it all the way up to the top. The collar feels as if stiff hands are squeezing at my neck, trying to choke the life out of me. I tolerate it for her. Everything is for her. The Aarons direct me to some trousers and a pair of shoes that go well with the look. They are such a fashion conscious bunch. The clothes I am wearing are like new. I have only ever worn them during life-altering occasions, such as weddings and funerals. They're fitting for the night that's ahead.

'How do I look?' I ask the room.

'You need to do more with your hair than just wash it,' says David Bowie as he steps out of my bath tub. He reaches a rock star hand out for my hair. 'Do you mind if I …'

'Oh, by all means.'

David Bowie's mismatched eyes assess what is in front of him as he turns hair stylist and drags a comb through my tangled head of hair. He applies some Brylcreem and continues to comb it through until I resemble a Wall Street investment banker in the eighties.

'To be successful you have to look successful,' he says as he applies the finishing touches. The Aarons nod their matching Wall Street heads in approval.

'She'll definitely fuck you now,' says one of them. 'We'd fuck us.'

'I'd fuck you,' says David Bowie.

'Thanks, David Bowie. That means a lot.'

David Bowie is such a nice guy.

I give myself the once-over while I douse my neck with a strongly scented after shave. It is probably the best that I can make myself look given my natural limitations, and probably the best that I have looked in quite some time. You can scream my name without any fear of guilt now, ladies. I am as ready to see Jane as I am ever going to be. The only problem is getting to her with what little is left of my sanity intact. The prospect of taking Dublin Bus for the fourth time in one day almost sends me running to vomit up what little of the roast beef dinner I ate. No one should ever have to suffer that. The Aarons are well ahead of me on that score.

'There's a car in the driveway. It's not like the old lady is going to miss it.'

'But I don't drive.'

'That's a minor detail. How hard could it be?'

They're right. Fuck public transport. Fuck Dublin Bus. Fuck all of the orange skinned, heroin-shooting, shit-scrape talking, saggy-faced people that ride on it. Tonight I am riding in style. I thank me for the help that I gave myself and run down to the kitchen, excited for the first time in a long time.

'I'm taking the car,' I say to my mother as I take the keys out of her cold pocket. 'I'll have it back to you as soon as I can.'

Driving is not so hard. Millions of people do it. I've sat in the passenger's seat all my life and watched my mother go through the motions a million times. Some of it is bound to have seeped in by some sort of osmosis. All I have to do is move it from point A to point B. I am no longer the passenger now though. I am in the driver's seat, a man in charge of his own destiny. Jane will have to be impressed when she sees me roll up in my very own Renault.

I open the car door and sit into the unfamiliar leather of the driver's seat, wrapping my fingers firmly around the steering wheel. My knuckles turn white with the strength of my nervous grip. Tentatively, I put the key in the ignition and give it a turn. The engine roars to life and the car gently vibrates all around me. Joe Dolan sings in my ears from the car speakers and I happily turn him off, killing off another piece of my mother in the process. So far, so good. I look down at the pedals and gently press my foot against the one I believe to be the accelerator. The car seems to take an eternity, but it does move. It just moves very, very slowly. I have barely outrun the snail beside the back tyre before the engine cuts out.

'Fuck.'

Let's give this another shot, shall we? I turn the key and put more pressure on the pedal. It still moves about as fast as an aids-riddled sloth, and the engine is making strange sounds. They are sounds I know not to be normal from my many times as a passenger. I look to the gear stick and wonder if that would help. I tap into the knowledge from all of the driving games I've played on the Playstation and I shift the gearstick into what I believe to be first. I see an immediate improvement and the car takes off before I can even get my bearings. I forget where the brake is and quickly take my foot off the accelerator as I rapidly approach a neighbour's car in the driveway opposite to mine. Even without my foot on the accelerator, the car's momentum is too fast to stop a collision. I turn the steering wheel aggressively, but the steering wheel doesn't work the way I always assumed it would. I crash gently into my neighbour's car, and the seatbelt holds me firmly in place as my body jerks forward on impact. Thankfully, my neighbour's car has no alarms that would alert nearby people to my blunder. I try my hand at reversing. The steering wheel still doesn't want to obey my commands but I still manage to stubbornly clear enough space to drive forward and away from the crash site. It's a stop-start process, but eventually I am on my way in an unsteady line. Just like a video game, I remind myself. Just like a video game. I am not even close to obeying the rules of the road, but I'm doing it. I'm driving. The only traffic I pass is the number seven bus as it picks up a stop load of evening passengers heading home after a long day at work. I give them all the finger as I sail majestically past. I am so invested in giving them the finger that I don't see the streetlamp right in front of me. The streetlamp wears my car as a neck tie as the number seven bus over takes me. A little kid gives me the finger from its passing window. I get out of the car and brush the glass off of me.

'I guess it was harder than we thought,' says the Aaron in the rear-view mirror.

Luckily, the number seven bus stop is right across the street.

CHAPTER FOURTEEN

'Lizards,' says the crazy man sitting beside me on the bus.

'Excuse me?'

'That's who runs the government. Lizards. They wear the faces of people. I watched a documentary about it.'

'I think this is my stop,' I say as I push the button.

'That's just what a lizard would say. I'm onto you. Go back to your lizard pit, you fucking gecko!'

Lizard-themed obscenities are hurled at my back as I get off the bus as fast as I can. Thankfully, it really is my stop. Jane's house is right in front of me. I stand there looking at it for a while under the pale glow of an emerging moon. I scan the perimeter, looking for any signs of activity. There are no cars in the driveway, so it would be safe to assume that Mr. Average has not yet come home. I wonder how much time I will have before he does. There's one light in the house still on. I know that she is there and that is where she waits for me. I feel more energised the more I think about it, like a kid who is next in line for the big ride at Disneyland. No more standing on the side-lines for Aaron Walsh. This is my moment. Time for me to breathe it in.

I am careful not to walk too heavily on the gravel as I approach the door. I bring my fist up to knock, but I just hold it there, hovering in mid-air without knocking. No, she should definitely not know that I am here. That would spoil the surprise, and I really want to see that look on her face when she realises I'm here. Moments like that are the only thing worth living for. Like a Victorian lady looking to preserve her virginity, I leave the front door behind and use the back entrance. I climb over the back garden wall in search of the window that is the furthest away from where Jane likely is. She has double-glazed windows, which are great for people who want to save money on their heating bills, but not so great for people looking to break into a property. I look around for options and notice that she has an unlocked shed by the back garden wall. Looking through the shed, I find a toolbox with a ballpoint hammer inside. I take the hammer and aim for the bottom-right corner of the double-glazed window. Two hard whacks in quick succession are enough to compromise the integrity of the glass and shatter it. I climb straight through the opening and find myself standing in her kitchen, on top of broken glass. I pause for a moment, waiting to hear if there are any sounds of movement in the house, but all is still. My presence has miraculously gone unnoticed and the surprise is still alive. This is going to be great, I know it.

My mind tries to remember where all the creaks in the stairs are from my last visit and I do my very best to avoid them. The closer I get to her room, the more activity I can hear. She is talking to someone, but the conversation is very one-sided, with the occasional pause. She's on the phone, I deduce. Too distracted to notice the sound of a smashed window. The only other sounds in the room are the 'yip-yip's of her dog, which surely knows that I am right outside the door, stalking, while its master talks on the phone, oblivious.

'Quiet, Roxy!' says Jane as she carries on with her phone conversation. But Roxy keeps on yipping and it's like having nails hammered into my forehead with every bark. I swear that dog must be Spanish.

I stay by the door and try to listen past the yipping. It would be bad etiquette of me to surprise her while she's still on the phone. So I wait and listen.

'I really need you to come home right now, Mark. I'm scared. I haven't been able to sit still since his visit.'

I hear a muffled response coming from the phone, but I can't quite make out what it says.

'Don't tell me to calm down! You weren't here. You didn't have to meet him. He's crazy! I can see it in his eyes. I don't care if you have to work late, just come home now, please. I wouldn't ask if it wasn't important.'

I edge closer to the doors opening and peer around the corner. Roxy has her teeth bared and is straining to get out of her master's arms. Jane keeps a firm hold of her, desperate for the comfort the rat-like, fluffy thing provides.

'If you don't come back home tonight, don't bother coming back home at all!'

She hangs up the phone in anger and tosses it onto the bed. Her body heaves as she silently sobs and hugs the rat thing. With her back turned, I creep into the room, ever so gently, and snatch her phone from the bed, putting it into my pocket. Roxy is beside herself with rage and is outright barking at me non-stop now, but it doesn't matter anymore. There is no more need for secrecy.

'Relationship trouble?' I ask.

She jumps back a full five feet in shock, dropping Roxy to the floor. Roxy wastes no time in charging straight for my ankles, her little body eager for action. She latches on and I try to shake her off, but she has the single-minded determination that comes with being a small-brained creature. I let her chew into the flesh of my ankle and try to ignore the pain as I turn towards Jane.

'What the fuck are you doing in my house!?' she demands.

'I just wanted to apologise for earlier. I made a bit of a fool out of myself.'

Her eyes dart to the place where she threw her phone. I pull it out of my pocket.

'Looking for this? I felt it best if we had a private conversation. Just you and me … and Roxy.'

I lift my foot and Roxy has latched on so hard that she comes up with it, dangling from my ankle by her teeth.

'Does she treat all house guests this way?'

'Just the ones who break in.'

'Sorry about that. I'll pay for the window I smashed. I really wanted to surprise you. Are you surprised? You look surprised.'

'Get out of my house. I'll only tell you once.'

'That's disappointing. I thought you'd be happier. Especially after that phone call with … Mark, was it? From what I can tell, the guy treats you like shit. All you want is a little company from someone who loves you and what does he say? "Sorry babe, work is more important than our relationship." That's a man who doesn't know the value of what he has.'

'At least he's not a fucking psycho! What is even going through your head right now? This is far from okay, you must realise that!'

I calmly reach down and yank Roxy away from my ankle, scooping her up into my arms. She fights me and nips at my fingers but I hold her firmly by the throat as she snarls uselessly.

'You put her down! You put her down right now!'

I absently look down at my white socks. A growing dot of red expands on one of them where Roxy's teeth punctured my flesh. I can feel the subtle sting that lets me know this is reality. The inside is on the outside. I am a child again.

'I want you to meet my family, Jane. They're waiting for you right now if you'll come with me. I want to show you who I really am and clear up any misunderstanding.'

'Can you even hear yourself right now? You are talking like a crazy person. I'm not going anywhere with you. I want you to leave and never come back here. If you do that right now, I won't call the police.'

'I might be crazy, but crazy people need love too. I choose yours. I want your love and I'm going to have it.'

'You can't just take love from someone.'

'Can't I?'

'What are you going to do, rape me? If you come near me I will make you wish you hadn't. I'll kill you before you get a chance to finish.'

'Is that what you think of me? I'm not going to rape you, Jane. When the time comes for that you won't even put up a fight. For now I just want your heart.'

'Well you're not getting it, so go to hell you fucking freak!'

'I'm not a freak! I love you! Don't you get that?'

Roxy chomps down on my thumb as I lose myself to anger and the red mist descends.

'Fucking mutt!'

I drop Roxy to the floor and suck on my bloody thumb as Jane makes a run for the door. She throws all of her weight into shouldering me aside and we both tumble to the floor. I reach out to grab her, but Roxy gets between us and bites into my cheek, buying Jane time to get up and run.

'Enough!' I shout as I grab the dog and get back to my feet. I slam Roxy down to the ground with all of the force I can muster. She bounces high like a basketball and comes to a stop at my feet. While she is dazed I stomp with the heel of my foot. The high-pitched yelp reverberates through the entire house as her tiny, fragile spine is snapped in two. Jane stops running.

'Roxy! You son of a bitch!'

Jane charges me with everything she has. It is the most beautiful I have ever seen her and all it took for that passion was one dead dog. She smashes me with her fists and I stagger backwards.

'Bastard!'

She kicks me in the ribs.

'Bastard!'

She headbutts me on the bridge of the nose.

'Bastard!'

She throws out another kick, but this time I catch it and counter with a punch to the gut.

'Bitch!'

She folds like an accordion, her body playing a wheezy tune of pain and suffering. I shove her over with my foot and start muttering.

'Love me. Love me. Love me. Loveme loveme lovemelovemeloveme …'

I keep shoving her further and further with my foot as she catches her breath.

'Love me.'

Shove.

'Love me.'

Shove. She hits the stair railings and uses them to pull herself up and face me. Her eyes are fierce and determined.

'Love yourself, because I fucking hate you.'

She spits in my face. Shove.

Down the stairs she falls with hips, elbows and spine bouncing in unnatural directions. She bounces all the way to the bottom and is still. A human slinky at the end of its journey.

'Are you still with me, Jane?'

'I … I can't move my legs,' her voice is frail and panicked. Dog and master both broken beneath my heel.

'You should be more careful. People die falling down stairs,' I say as I descend. 'It didn't have to be like this. We can fix everything, though. We can work through our problems. You need to trust that I love you and it will all be okay.'

'Oh, God.'

She tries to crawl away, her fingernails scraping against the hardwood floor as she pulls her entire bodyweight along. Her nails snap and bleed before I bring her to a stop by placing my foot on her broken back.

'Not so fast, missy. All I want from you now is one kiss. One kiss and I'll leave you alone forever.'

'Get … away.'

I flip her over and mount myself on top. There is no struggle anymore. I gaze longingly into her eyes and she gazes right back into mine. She doesn't look away.

'There's my girl.'

I lower myself and plant the sweetest of kisses upon the flesh of her lips. At the same time I slide a concealed knife into her stomach and twist. She gasps slightly as the knife penetrates. Tears roll down her cheeks as she accepts her fate. I look into her eyes and watch until she is no longer watching me back. It is the most intimate of moments. She really was beautiful.

A MOMENT FOR THE READER

How are we feeling, dear reader? Are you still with me? Are you feeling like an accomplice to my deeds? I can't begin to imagine what you must think of me. Jane Flannery was the last person you could root for in this story and now she is dead. Where is the hero in this piece? In short, there is none. But now you ask, where could we possibly go when there is no one to cheer and no hope for a happy ending? Welcome to life – you might have heard of it. You forget that this is my story and by reading it, it is now yours. We go where I choose to go and we are certainly going to go places. None of them will be good, but we will go there all the same.

It will only get worse from here. You might be wondering how that is even possible, but trust me, it does. I promise you that no one is safe. Not even you. You were probably expecting some light, easy read that you could kill in a few bus journeys when you picked up the contents of my mind. That was your mistake. Delve into the head of your average person and you will find that no one's mind is a light affair. We all have a certain potential for madness within us, so be careful what you take into your hands. Some ideas can make you lose everything you are.

Murder is really not that hard when you break it down. We have been killing and knocking the shit out of each other for thousands of years. We are built and programmed by nature to expire. We kill each other for resources, we kill each other for revenge, we kill each other for punishment, we kill each other for love, we kill each other to protect. We kill each other because we can. The most natural thing you can do besides fuck someone is kill them, because life and death are inseparable. It is how nature keeps us in check. We are at the top of the food chain, and with nothing to hunt us we would destroy this planet if left unchecked. That is why we have the urge to kill each other. We are our own balancing force.

Genghis Khan's Mongol empire massacred forty million people and wiped entire civilisations off the face of the Earth. His empire, at its peak, spanned a full quarter of the globe. This empire, built on murder and brutality, was one of the greatest things to ever happen to the planet. The lands that man had cultivated returned to the forest, and many tonnes of carbon dioxide were scrubbed from the atmosphere like at no other period in human history. All of this because of our natural impulse to kill. We act like murder is not civilised, when murder is our civilisation.

But we do like to pretend that we are more than mere beasts waiting for death on a lonely, isolated rock in space. So every now and then, when one of the population acts according to their primal nature, we will judge and punish them. People do this because it allows them to point a finger and say 'I'm not like that'. I can already feel you pointing your finger even now. You are hoping that someone you can identify with will come along and string me up, all so you can say that 'I am not you' with your outstretched finger.

We are a species of hypocrites that have become bloated on our own self-importance. A burden to our planet, because we seek to prevent the glorious self-destruction that nature has always intended for us. I suggest that you judge less and start doing your part to cull the herd. If someone out there is pissing you off, give it a try. You have my permission. You will be shocked at how easily your hand 'slips'. All murder takes is a nudge. If I nudge you enough then you may find out that you really are just like me.

CHAPTER FIFTEEN

In Jane's upstairs wardrobe I find a gigantic luggage bag. Being a typical woman, she probably felt the need to pack her entire life for a two-week trip at some point and needed the extra room. It is a great bag to pack a life into. I plan to pack Jane's into it, as she likely always intended. I drag it down the stairs with me while I sing.

Jane Flannery is no good,
Chop her up for fire wood,
If she doesn't do for that,
We'll feed her to the pussy cat.

'That was something my dad used to sing to me,' I say as I reach the bottom of the stairs.

'It was with my name instead of yours, of course. He wasn't clairvoyant. If he was he would have stopped me pushing that ladder. I bet that he really does wish he'd fed me to the pussy cat, wherever he is.'

I hook under Jane's armpits and heave her dead weight off the ground. Once I have her positioned over the bag, I gently guide her in and contort her shape until it fits. Nice and snug.

'I know that you probably have a lot of questions. The answer to most of them is boredom. Boredom ultimately guides everything I do. At least we're not bored now, are we? We'll see how long that lasts. Boredom is always lurking, waiting for its chance to make the interesting mundane. Sometimes it makes you act just to stave it off and you can't stop it. Blaise Pascal once said that all of humanity's problems stem from a man's inability to sit quietly in a room alone.'

Her eyes no longer look at me with disgust. Her eyes are whatever I imagine them to be and in this moment I am imagining to be full of love and understanding. She loves all of the deeds I have done and all of the sacrifices I have made in her name. She finally gets it, at long last, even though she's not in a position to say it. She is the reward for everything I've had to suffer. All the humiliation that I've had to endure.

'You want to know why you got my attention? You looked me in the eyes. I know that sounds like a simple thing, but it's not. People have always had trouble looking me in the eye. There's always been something about my gaze that unsettles them. Do you know how strange it is to have so many people talk to you every day and do their very best never to look you in the eye? It's like they are afraid I'll see them, or maybe they are afraid that they'll see me. Maybe they don't want to see the monster in their own reflections. Over a long enough timescale we're all monsters to someone.'

I zip the luggage bag up and Jane disappears from view. With great effort, I tilt the bag back onto its wheels and drag it into her front garden. I sit down on the porch beside her and catch my breath.

'I wasn't always this bad, you know. I kept it together for many years. All through my life I've heard people talk about me when they think I can't hear them. No one ever lets you be yourself. People always have to get together and decide what you are. They say what they think you are so often that you start to believe it. If so many people are saying it, then it must be true. When you start to believe it, you start to become it. I am what people have made me. They have talked me into existence because they can't bear to look me in the eyes.'

I start to wonder if Jane can even hear me. Do my words reach her across the void, or do they die in the wind? Is she even listening with her mortal ears, or with something far greater and unknowable? Either way, it comforts me to speak to her without a filter. It's rare to feel so free.

'You're actually not the first Jane that I've had a crush on. There was a girl called Jane Griffin in my secondary school days. Jane was pretty – not as pretty as you, but pretty. She was almost too much for my teenage self to handle. I thought about her all the time. Fucked her in my imagination constantly. By this stage of my life people had gotten what they call "the vibe" off me and I was forced to sit alone at lunch. I used to be able to dominate and force people to tolerate my company, but gradually age gave them the confidence to have a backbone and stand up to me. So every day I would sit alone and watch her, thinking about what it would be like if she one day decided to turn in my direction and acknowledge my existence, but she never did. She knew I was there; she knew I was looking. But she never gave me the satisfaction of looking back.

'One day, I worked up the courage to speak to her. I figured that if we talked she would have to look at me, and if she looked at me then maybe she'd love me. Stupid, right? She just looked right past me and didn't say a single word in response. She turned her back to me and continued talking to her friends, like I wasn't even there. You know what she said to her friends about me? She said, "He'll have to rape someone to lose his virginity." She didn't even wait for me to walk away first. Oh, how they laughed. They all laughed at my expense. They laughed at me, but they still wouldn't dare look at me. If only they could see me now. I bet I wouldn't be quite so invisible. I bet that they wouldn't be laughing.'

The taxi that I've ordered pulls up in front of the house. Not this time, Dublin Bus.

'You're going to set it right for me, Jane.'

The driver gets out of the car and moves towards the bag.

'Let me help you with that.'

He has it before I can stop him. The weight is more than he anticipated.

'Jesus. What have you got in here? A dead body?'

I offer no explanation as my face goes pale.

'Just kidding,' he says with a laugh as he heaves it into the boot of the car with my assistance.

'Are you going to the airport?' he asks, on account of the large bag.

'No,' I say. 'We're going home.'

'We?'

I smile at him nervously.

'I'm going home.'

CHAPTER SIXTEEN

I sit in the back of the taxi, away from the driver. If I am paying a premium price for my transport then I am not sitting up front with the hired man. I expect the full chauffeur experience of being driven by someone in my temporary employ. It's a shame that the division of front and back does little to deter any conversation attempts. Taxi drivers love to talk and if you don't talk back to them, they'll just talk at you.

'I went to Japan last year,' says the taxi driver. 'Weird place. Have you ever been?'

'Nope,' I say with disinterest.

'You should go if you get the chance. They have vending machines that sell used panties. Can you believe that? Not that I bought any, but they have them. Just saying. Makes you wonder what kind of sick bastard would want used panties. Anyway, I went to the Mt. Fuji region and at the base of the mountain I visited the Aokigohara forest. You ever hear of it?'

'Can't say that I have.'

'The "Sea of Trees" they call it. It's the second most popular suicide destination on Earth, after the Golden Gate Bridge. I don't know what it is about the Japanese but they sure love killing themselves. They had those kamikaze pilots back in the war and those other blokes that would fall on their swords. I'm not suicidal myself, I just wanted to see it and understand it. There was such a creepy aura in that forest, knowing that so many people have died there. It was eerily quiet – I mean, not even the wildlife made a sound. It's like places know when bad things have happened. I once read that they have a guy who patrols the area looking for bodies. Can you imagine that? I wonder what it's like to be surrounded by so much death.'

'I wouldn't know.'

'I'm just happy driving a taxi. Worst I have to deal with is some drunk getting sick in the back seat.'

Something catches the driver's attention outside the window.

'Ha. Looks like people in Ireland are trying to kill themselves too.'

It's the car that I crashed into a lamppost. Two Garda Síochána surround it; one of them takes note of the license plate in her notepad. They are beginning the process of loading the car onto a truck and getting it off the road. My heart jumps up into my throat and refuses to be swallowed as we pass by. The Garda with the notepad makes eye contact with me and stares into my soul. I start to feel that time is perhaps growing short. The license plate number in her notepad might as well be a ticking clock. All I need is one night.

The taxi arrives at my house and I pay the driver what I owe him and nothing more. His response is to not help me as I heave the bag out of the trunk of his car. My poor back. Every fresh murder puts it under strain. With every heave of a dead body, my living one protests. It doesn't need the use of my mouth to make itself heard. It says that my muscles have limits and that I should chill the fuck out, because I obviously don't know what I'm doing. 'Take up origami or some shit instead,' it tells me; 'Paper doesn't weigh a thing.' I tell my body to shove its opinion up our collective arse. This is happening, whether it likes it or not. I have gone too far down this road to quit over a little grunt work.

I get Jane to the door and set the bag down. Hard-earned sweat beads on my forehead, but is mercifully cooled by the crisp, Irish air. I watch the taxi disappear into the distance, leaving Jane and me alone once more.

'I was never meant for hard labour,' I say to the bag containing Jane's body. 'You can probably tell that I don't do much of it. My greatest asset has always been my mind and I usually let that do the heavy lifting for me. I have an imagination like no other. Oh, the things I can imagine. You wouldn't believe some of it. I firmly believe that if you can imagine something happening, then you can make it happen. If you have a good imagination then you can fake all the other bullshit things in life. Imagi-nation is all you really need. I'm going to keep imagining things, Jane. My imagination is always preferable to this reality. We are all going to play our parts, because my imagination is going to make it happen.'

I give the bag a reassuring pat as I fumble for the house keys.

'Poor thing. What a night you've had. You must be very tired. We'll get you to a bed soon, but not quite yet. My family are simply dying to meet you.'

I open the door and everything is as I left it. A silence hangs over the air; it is different to your average silence. It's a silence that speaks and says that something happened here. It speaks without having to say a word at all. Silence is a teller of many secrets for those who have an ear to listen. This house is my Sea of Trees. It is a place that knows something has happened. I put the thought of it out of my mind.

'Sorry about the mess. Things were a bit crazy here,' I say into the sentient silence as I wrestle the improvised body bag through the door. The wheels pull up the welcome mat as I drag them along, leaving the invitation obscured to any who should follow. I shut the door on the outside world and sigh with relief. The hard part is over. Now that Jane is out of public view, it's time to make her feel at home. I unzip the bag and reveal my prize. Jane almost looks as if she is sleeping peacefully when the light hits her face.

'Rise and shine, my love.'

I pull Jane up to her feet and manipulate her body like a puppet master with his marionette. My hands and my will are the strings by which she is guided.

'Mum, Rachel! I have someone that I'd like for you to meet,' I shout into the kitchen.

Jane is marched into the kitchen, walking with the aid of my toes. She is proudly displayed to my family like a prom date ahead of the big dance. They say nothing, of course, but I'd like to think that they are left speechless that their Aaron has brought home such a treasure. Aaron, whose eyes no one could look into, had gone and got himself a catch. It's a true underdog story of guy gets girl against all odds. They will probably make a film about it someday. I wonder who will play me.

'No need for any of you to get up. Jane and I will be joining you for dinner.'

I drop Jane and she folds over, making a meaty thud against the kitchen floor. I pull out a chair before picking her back up again.

'Sorry darling. I was trying to be a gentleman and forgot how delicate you are. You'll feel fine once you have a chair under you. I hope you like roast beef.'

I place her carefully on the chair and tilt her face up towards my mother's mangled eye. She stares at it with her own vacant fascination. I think about how I have given my mother a permanent conversation piece and struggle to contain my laughter. 'What's with the eye?' people will ask her, and she'll say, 'Funny story, that. All I can say is, put your cutlery away when my Aaron is around.' We'd all have a laugh at that. An inside joke for all the family.

'I know how you're always complaining about having to do everything around here, mum, so I'll fix Jane a plate myself.'

I leave the girls to chat amongst themselves and take a sharp knife to the dry hunk of roast beef sitting atop the stove. I wish that I had something better to offer, but this is all that there is. I serve the plate up to Jane and hope that she doesn't turn her nose up at it.

'Bon appétit.'

I take a seat by her side, facing my mother with her funny eye, and my sister with her punctured face. They are all at peace and silent. Not a single, solitary sound disturbs the room.

'This is nice.'

A buzz of wings intrudes on the ceremony as a fly lands on my sister's face. No hand moves to swat it away. She just lets it sit there, taunting the room with its shit-stained legs rubbing together with glee. It climbs over her eyelid and onto the surface of her eye. Trying to move as little as possible, I roll up a newspaper that is sitting on the table and eye the little intruder up. Carefully I take aim and – THWACK! – the little bastard is dead. The blow jerks my sister's head to the left and she starts to slide in her seat. At first she slides only a little, until gravity does the rest of the work for her and she crumples to the floor in a heap.

'Aw shit. How about we just eat? This is getting kind of awkward.'

There are no objections, so I fork the cold roast beef into my mouth and swallow it like a duck, as fast as possible, not pausing to savour the taste that has already been evaporated in the oven. I look up and see that the others are not touching their plates. Not a single gravy-soaked scrap goes into their mouths.

'Yeah, it's not the best, is it?'

But I can't get the silence at the table out of my head. It hangs there, refusing to be ignored. Stupid fucking taxi driver talking about that stupid fucking forest. I close my eyes and focus on my chewing and the sound it makes in the confines of my head. The silence disappears, unable to follow the retreat into myself. All I can hear is saliva and teeth on beef, and my nose breathing in a steady rhythm. I focus my imagination on what I want to make happen, and I open my eyes. There is no more silence. There are no more corpses. There are just three women getting to know each other, all of them happy to be in my company.

'It's great to finally meet you, Jane,' says my mother. She hasn't looked this good in years.

'Thank you so much for having me,' says Jane. 'Aaron has told me so much about you guys.'

'Not too much, I hope. I can sometimes be an insufferable bitch, who doesn't know what a good son she has.'

'Yes,' Rachel agrees. 'We give Aaron an awful time and try his patience on a regular basis. Makes me wonder how he puts up with us.'

I say, 'Mum, you might be interested to know that Jane writes children's novels.'

Her interest perks up at this. She is visibly impressed.

'You don't say. A writer at my dinner table.'

'Pretty cool, right? It's kind of like a form of immortality, to have your words on a page for the world to read.'

'Oh please, darling. You'll embarrass me,' says Jane. 'Really it's just a hobby that got out of hand. Now young girls are getting notions.'

'We wouldn't want that,' says my mother, offended at the idea. 'It is every woman's duty to look after the men in their life.'

'Don't worry, Mrs. Walsh. My writing days are behind me. I have Aaron now, and that's all I need.'

'Glad to hear it,' says my mother, regaining her composure. 'What I'm most interested in, however, is if you have what it takes to look after my Aaron. I only have one son and I want to see him happy.'

Jane smiles at this and takes me warmly by the hand.

'You don't need to worry about that, either. I plan to see to everything he needs. It's not often that a man like this comes along. Just this evening, Aaron was nice enough to return my laptop to me. The very first thing I did when I got it back was look up deep-throat techniques. I want all of him down there, his cock ramming against the walls of my throat. I want him to fuck my throat so hard that I gag with pleasure and cry tears of joy.'

'That reminds me of a time …' my sister begins.

'Now, now, Rachel,' I cut off. 'Jane doesn't want to hear your stories about being a cock-sucking whore. She is just expressing her desire for me to cum in her mouth.'

My mother weighs in on the subject.

'I find the best way to deep-throat is to start by gripping the base of the shaft. Swallow until you gag, pause and breathe, and then swallow some more. You'll get the hang of it.'

Jane grips hard at my thigh while making intense and lusty eye contact.

'I wish you could fuck me right now, right here on this table. You know I want it bad, Aaron. You could bend me over this table and put it in my arse.'

'Patience, darling. My family is in the room.'

'I want them to see. I want them to see how much I love you fucking me. I want your mother to see how well I treat you. I want her to see you happy.'

'That sounds great, but I think that our first time should be special, don't you? If you're still of a mind to later, we can destroy this kitchen with our bodies. I'll even fuck you on top of the roast beef. Your cunt can give it moisture.'

'Oh, you know how to get me going.'

'Get a room, you two!' says Rachel.

'Oh we will, sis, you don't need to worry about that. You might want to put some ear plugs in later, 'cause Jane has told me that she's a screamer.'

Rachel rolls her eyes but is smiling at the same time.

'Fine. As long as you give me a little niece or nephew.'

'There's a good chance of that. I didn't even stop to buy condoms. No point practicing safe sex when you are not a safe person to begin with. Everything is dangerous where I'm concerned.'

Jane tries a little bit of her meal and politely holds back a grimace in view of my mother.

'You know what, fuck the food. This is a celebration. We shouldn't be eating, we should be dancing.'

I jump out of my chair with a hop and a skip and run over to the speaker jack with my phone.

'Any requests?' I ask of the room.

'How about some Amanda Palmer?' Jane suggests.

'Not really my style, but if it's what the lady wants, it will be what the lady gets. Do you see how much I compromise for you? What a pair we'll make.'

I do a quick search online and find an Amanda Palmer playlist. I hit shuffle and a song called 'What's the use of won'drin'?' begins to play. The summary says that it is a cover of a song from the musical *Carousel*. The opening of the song begins and I offer my hand to Jane with a bow.

'M'lady, may I please have this dance?'

Jane giggles to herself and places her hand in mine.

'I'm all yours, good sir.'

The song has a slow tempo so I pull her in close, looking lovingly into her eyes, my fingers interlocked with hers. It might just be my imagination, but I am better at this dancing thing than I give myself credit for. I can feel her heart swoon as I dip her and pull her up again in time to the music.

Common sense may tell you,

That the ending will be sad,

And now's the time to break and run away,

But what's the use of won'dring,

If the ending will be sad?

He's your fella and you love him,

There's nothing more to say.

'You know something, Jane. I actually like this one.'

'Why?'

'I like it, is all. She's not whining about her feelings for once. It helps that she didn't write it, I suppose.'

'Why?'

'What do you mean why? I just told you.'

But Jane has stopped dancing. Her feet drag across the floor and her weight hangs limply in my arms. It is me and her corpse once more, but her voice comes from somewhere far away.

'Why?'

I look to the floor where my sister lays crumpled. Her neck turns ever so slightly to look at me and ask one question.

'Why?'

The wounded eye in my mother's head swivels like a compass arrow, but the rest of her is still. Four red fork marks find my face and ask one question.

'Why?'

I drop Jane to the floor, and as she falls she asks the question.

'Why?'

'Shut up, all of you!'

Amanda Palmer begins to sing through the speakers.

Why? Why? Why?

Why? Why? Why?

I rip the speakers out of the socket and smash them against the wall. There are no more questions after that. Everything has returned to the dead silence of before, which now doesn't seem so bad. A forest of corpses planted in my kitchen.

'I think it is time that Jane and I said goodnight. I am very ashamed of you all for making a scene like this. I bring a girl home and this is how you all behave! We'll talk about this in the morning, but right now I am going to fuck my woman and show her what to do with that smart mouth of hers. Come on, Jane, we're leaving!'

I take her corpse by the hand and begin to drag it along the kitchen floor, losing any kind of delicate touch that I once had. Once we hit the stairs, her head bounces with every step. I keep dragging her up with all my strength, one exhausting thump at a time. I speak to her in between heavy, wheezing breaths.

'You just keep your mouth shut now.'

THUMP!

'This is going to be a night that neither of us will forget.'

THUMP!

'I'm going to look you in the eyes while I fuck you. I'm going to look at you, looking at me!'

THUMP!

We conquer the stairs and I start the new obstacle of pulling her along the drag-resistant carpet and into my bedroom.

'Here we are, dear. The place where the magic happens. I hope that you're ready for what I'm going to do to you.'

I heave her up and throw her onto the bed. Her head bounces and whips her hair back over her face. I start to unbutton my shirt.

'Shit! I forgot the Vaseline! You wait right there!'

I charge into the upstairs bathroom and knock everything aside in my search for Vaseline while muttering to myself.

'Fuck that bitch. I'm gonna fuck you, Jane. Fuck you. Gonna fuck you. Fuck … AHA!'

I grip my sweaty fingers around a Vaseline tub and march back to the bedroom triumphant.

'Gonna fuck you. Fuck you good. Gonna fuck you. Fuck you.'

I am frothing at the mouth, every word flying through the air on drops of spittle. The Vaseline gets thrown on the bed as I lose the rest of the clothes, ripping them off in my urgency. Finally, I am naked, my Vaseline-greased cock as erect as it has ever been and ready to penetrate its life into death. It is finally going to happen and I will be a virgin no more. I pounce onto the bed, controlled by a primal lust. She loses her dress. She loses her panties. I am a hair's breadth away from inserting six inches when a voice stops me cold.

'What the fuck do you think you're doing?'

I slowly look up from the dead body that has been begging to be fucked all night and lock eyes with the translucent ghost of that same body. Jane Flannery has come back from the land of the dead for the sole purpose of cock blocking, and man, she looks pissed.

'Well, shit.'

A MOMENT FOR JANE FLANNERY

There once was an awkward boy called Nathan and he was my first friend in the whole world. Nathan barely measured past his father's kneecap, but that was to be expected, given his young age. He often wore the dungarees that his parents dressed him in and he carried a slingshot in his back pocket. Geographically, there was only a corner that separated us and every day he would turn that corner on his trike and pull to a stop outside my parents' driveway. He would go that far and no further, as he feared my older brothers answering the door. They were hulking giants compared to his tiny frame. It was a strain on his neck to even look at them in all of their intimidating, older-boy glory.

'Jane!' he would shout in the general direction of the house. This was his way of knocking. 'Jaaaaaane!!!'

My parents would groan and my brothers would curse at the familiar, morning sound of my name being shouted to the heavens. I have to admit that I kind of liked it. It's not often that people shout your name to the world.

'Your boyfriend's here,' my family would say, but I didn't understand. A boyfriend was what my Barbie had. This was just Nathan. I would meet him at the edge of the driveway after his voice had gone hoarse from shouting and we'd go play. There were always all sorts of games and fun to be had, and at the end of it all we would go back to our homes covered in enough dirt to horrify our parents.

When we were old enough, we ended up going to different schools, but Nathan would still turn that corner and shout my name, long after his fear of my brothers had passed. I thought that we would be friends forever, that time could never change us; but ultimately, time always has a say in how things progress.

People outside of the friendship started telling us things. We were old enough and we needed to know, or so they said. I couldn't roll around in the mud anymore because that's not what girls do. He couldn't play with my dolls anymore because that's not what boys do. In my school, the boys wouldn't let me join their games. A girl would just ruin things if you were to believe what they said. A wall went up between me and the opposite sex, and then one day, when I looked up at lunch, I noticed all of my friends were now exclusively girls talking exclusively about 'girl things'. A similar thing happened to Nathan, only his friends were boys and they talked about 'boy things'. We had started our friendship equal and the same, but then people told us that we weren't and our paths diverged.

Nathan stopped turning that corner. I waited to hear the sound of my name every day, but it was no longer shouted. I thought that maybe it was time that I turned the corner for a change.

'Nathan!' I shouted outside of his house. 'Naaaaaathaaaaaaan!!!'

Nathan appeared in his bedroom window and looked down at me on the street. I smiled and waved at him, but he did not smile or wave in return. He closed his blinds and left me standing on the street alone. I ran home and cried because I had lost the rarest of friends. A friend that knew me before people defined me. They are not something that you can pick off of a tree. For years I went down the girl path and he went down the boy path, and we did it all without speaking to each other.

We were reunited again when we attended the same secondary school. I didn't know if we could pick up the friendship where we left off, or whether that chapter in our lives was dead for good. Part of me secretly hoped, but I wasn't quite sure how to behave around him anymore. Time had made strangers of us. I was still thinking with a mind of childlike innocence and naiveté, but the rules had changed yet again, without me even knowing it. He didn't ignore me anymore, and I was glad of that, but there was something different about the way he looked at me. I was simply happy that he was talking to me again, even if it was just a word or two in between classes.

I was invited to a party when I was fifteen, at my friend Barbara's place.

Her parents had flown to Paris for the week and left her behind in the house, alone, without any adult supervision. Most of my school year attended that party and I drank my first alcohol that night. I was on my third can of beer – and in the process of discovering that I was an extreme lightweight – when I heard a sound that I hadn't heard in quite some time, coming from outside the house.

'Jane! Jaaaaaaane!!!'

Barbara went to the front door and demanded that Nathan shut up and come inside before the neighbours complained.

'There she is!' he said when he saw me. He was already drunk.

The party resumed, as parties do, and I got to chatting with Nathan about the old times. Maybe the alcohol played a part, but we were fully comfortable in each other's company for the first time in a long time. It was nice. I had really missed him.

We went outside for a smoke and took a walk around Barbara's gigantic back garden, gazing up at the stars. We laughed and joked until we were obscured behind some trees. Nathan used the opportunity to lean in for a kiss, but I pulled away from him.

'What are you doing?'

He seemed a little nervous, like he had thought about this moment a lot.

'I just wanted to kiss you,' he said. 'Is that so bad?'

I didn't know what to say. I had never kissed a boy before and I never considered that Nathan might want to kiss me. He leaned in again and I didn't pull away this time. Our lips met and it felt all wrong. It was not what I imagined a first kiss feeling like. I just didn't have feelings for him in that way. I broke from him and took a step back.

'Sorry, Nathan, but you're like a brother to me.'

He closed the distance and groped at my boob.

'I want to be more.'

'Stop that!' I said as I knocked his hand away, but he responded by forcefully pinning me up against a tree. The look in his eye at that moment was like nothing I had ever seen before.

'Just once. Please. I've thought about it so long.'

His pants were coming down and I could feel what was underneath pressed up against me and growing up my leg. A snake on a thigh branch.

'No!' I shouted, but he wasn't hearing it. We started life as equals, but now I was just the object that used to be his friend.

'I said no!'

I reached up with my thumb and jammed it into his eye, just enough to make him back up and think twice. While he was bent over and clutching at his injured eye, I picked up the largest branch I could find and held it over him like a baseball bat. He squinted up and saw me there, towering over him. In all the times he had thought about that moment, this was probably the last possible way he thought it would play out.

'Jane?'

'Nathan!'

I swung the branch and it was a homerun. His head was knocked right out of the park. Nathan fell to the grass unconscious. It was the last time I ever let him shout my name. That day I turned a corner of my own.

CHAPTER SEVENTEEN

'Murderer!' shouts the spirit, pointing her outstretched finger in my direction. The corpse beneath my naked body becomes less interesting with the sudden arrival of its former occupant. She can't possibly be there. I killed her with my own two hands. I close my eyes and open them again, but she is still there. Still just as real.

'No,' I say to myself in disbelief. The word escapes from me and the spirit delights in it.

'Yes,' it responds, a smug smile crossing its ghostly face.

Invisible hands reach and lift me up off the bed. I look around and my eyes can't believe what they are seeing. I am floating in mid-air, with nothing to support me. I am a living impossibility faced with a dead impossibility. The ghost of Jane stares me down and I fly through the air. I fly and crash into the nearest wall, all the air driven out of my lungs on impact.

'Rapist!' she shouts. I try to get my bearings, but I am lifted again and flung into another wall like a rag doll.

'Filth!'

I struggle for breath as I feel an unnatural tightening within my throat.

'You're not really here,' I manage to say in between shallow breaths. The tightening stops. Jane walks to stand over me and look down, a wry smile upon her lips.

'Then where am I?' she asks. Her tone is mocking. I get back to my feet so that I can face her like a man, and say the only thing that could possibly be real.

'You're in my head.'

A swift drop in temperature causes my blood to cool. The air is as cold as ice, my breath visible upon it. I shiver and rub my arms for warmth as goosebumps rise up all across my flesh. Jane takes a step closer and stares me down with her opaque eyes.

'Guess again,' she says in a voice as cold as the air between us. I nod my understanding to her and the temperature returns to normal. Her assault on me ceases, now that she has my full attention, though I notice that her appearance is not as vibrant as when she first appeared. I make a mental note of that fact and do a slow circle of the spectre that stands before me. It is Jane just as I remember her, yet different. Her shape and outline are vividly clear, but I can see through her as if looking through a window that has been covered in a fresh morning frost.

'This can't be,' I mutter. 'It's a fiction invented by cowards too afraid to deal with how temporary they are. It's not real.'

'Saying something doesn't make it so,' she teases. 'You think you get answers? You don't. You have no power here. All you get is judgement, and believe me when I say that judgement is coming for you.'

An image flashes into my head from an outside source. I see my own entrails hanging bloody from my still-living body. I scream as hands with no face reach out from the darkness to pull more of my insides to the outside. I shake the image loose and look at Jane. She is too smug for her own good. I reach out to touch her ghost-flesh and the smugness disappears. She recoils away from me as if I could possibly kill her twice.

'Don't you dare touch me!'

I raise my hands into the air.

'I promise if you promise.' I offer a smug smile of my own. She offers me nothing but silence, but I can work with that.

'I can't believe it,' I say. 'There actually is an afterlife.'

'Not any that you'll want to visit,' she says with a smile. 'There is a special kind of hell waiting for you, Aaron Walsh. You will pay for every life you have ruined, ten times over.'

'So I gather.'

It is my turn to be silent. The thoughts provoked by this revelation are loud, and they drown me in an ocean of self-doubt. Life, death, and afterlife co-existing under the same roof. A lifetime of certain thinking within my very core has been challenged and defeated. I don't care so much that there is an afterlife, I care that I was wrong. It eats me up. If there was a way for me to kill the afterlife, I'd do it right now. The dead should stay buried.

'Why have you come back here, Jane? Did you miss me that much?'

'I'm here to put a stop to all of this.'

'What do you care? I thought that I had no power here.'

'You don't.'

'People with no power don't need to be stopped. Have you just come to torment me with your knowledge of the grave? That there is something out there that I didn't actually know? Well, you've succeeded. This is actually kind of fucking with my head right now.'

'I came to preserve what is left of my dignity.'

'You're trying to save the meat? That's what all of this is about?' I laugh at the absurdity. 'I will take my pleasure from it. You can't stop that. It's all still so pointless for me, even with the knowledge you've brought. You've already made it clear that there is no reward waiting for me, so I might as well make one for myself now, while things are still in my control.'

'You try it and I'll hurt you. You know that I can.'

'Why not join in? We could have a three-way. Me, your body, and your ghost in one glorious trinity. I bet that's something that's never been done. We should do it for that reason alone. Think of the history that could be made. We'd get to know what Neil Armstrong felt like when he was the first man to walk on the moon. Don't you want to walk with me, Jane? One small step for all of us, in the name of discovery. Things have gotten very interesting and the interesting moments are so rare.'

'You can't be serious,' she says with disgust.

'Do you think I am a man who jokes about such things? Is it even possible for me to touch you anyway?'

I move quickly to touch her arm before she can react, but my hand passes right through her body. A shudder travels up the length of my arm and down to the base of my spine. The feel of her is like dipping a hand into cold bath water.

'You're already in a world of shit and you want to dig your hole even further. You're hopeless.'

'Even a man on death row gets his last meal. Would you really deny me the thing that I want most in this world before you condemn my soul?

That's a bit cruel, don't you think?'

I pass my hand through her again and take a liking to the shuddery sensation. She jumps back away from me, not liking where things are going.

'So, how about it?' I ask her. 'Why don't you climb back into that body and I'll fuck you both good.'

'If you think for one second that I would ever fuck you after what you've done, then you are far more delusional than I think you realise.'

'Can't blame a man for trying. It will be just as fun with you watching, anyway.'

'I'm warning you. Don't even think about it.'

'I like it rough, but somehow I don't think that you have what it takes. I think that I have more power than you would have me believe.'

I can see her face turn red with anger as I climb back on top of the bed and lay hands on her dead body. I caress the tender flesh of her breast.

'Get off of me!'

'Show me who has the power and maybe I might.'

I mount her and it is more than her skin that is cold. The temperature drops once more as I hold my cock over her dead, naked crotch. I stimulate myself to keep the feeling of lust alive. The lights flicker on and off repeatedly with a menacing electric hum. They are threatening further consequence if I don't cease and desist.

'You'll need more than party tricks. What else are you going to do? Rattle some chains and make spooky noises?'

A book flies from the shelf and cracks me in the head, followed by another, and another. She hits me with Stephen King and Charles Bukowski. A Neil Gaiman hardcover punches me right in the mouth. Haruki Murakami works the body. Drops of blood fall from my mouth and stain the sheets. I bring a hand up to my lip, more in surprise than pain. Her invisible force takes hold of me and throws me to the ceiling, before letting me crash back down to the bed. Chips of paint and plaster rain down on my head as an angry earthquake shakes everything around me. I start to wonder if maybe I have bitten off more than I can chew, but then everything falls silent and still. The chaos is over as quickly as it started.

I look over to Jane's ghost and she is more faded now than she was before. She is barely an outline, and that outline is an exhausted one. I can see the concentration on her face as she struggles to keep her form intact. She is a flickering projection of a person. I laugh at how pathetic she looks. I can't stop myself.

'Look at you, all out of breath. I knew you didn't have it in you. I thought that you came here to stop me, not start a book club.'

She bursts into tears and crouches down to the floor. I'm not really sure how to react, so I just stare at her dumbfounded and ask the first stupid question that comes to my lips.

'Are … you okay?'

'No, I'm not okay, you fucking asshole! I'm dead and you killed me, and now you are going to violate what's left of me. Does any of that sound okay to you?'

'Well, of course it sounds bad when you put it like that.'

'I had so much left that I wanted to do. I was just starting to make progress. The books were selling well. My blog was taking off. My name was starting to get out there and people wanted to hear what I had to say, but then I had to go to the wrong computer store.'

'You've still got plenty to, um, live for, I guess. Think of all the celebrities you can meet. Elvis, Marilyn Monroe, Joe Dolan. Well, maybe not Joe Dolan, but you get the picture. Does everyone sit on a cloud up there or what?'

The sobbing continues and I shift about uncomfortably where I sit. Nothing makes me more awkward than someone crying in my presence.

'Yeah, who wants a cloud, right? The descriptions of heaven always sounded dull and boring to me. Sitting on a cloud in a white robe, playing a harp. When was the last time you ever saw anyone playing a harp? Hey, I know that you said that you're not here to answer my questions, but would you mind answering just one for me?'

She looks up from her sobbing, her curiosity piqued.

'What?'

'What is it like to die? I've watched enough people do it, but it's not the same as feeling it. I want to know.'

She stops crying and her eyes harden. I am the one who has to look away for once. I don't like what I see in the depths of those eyes. They know things that are still yet a mystery to me. I am not a man who likes to be in the dark.

'Do you really want to know?' she asks, and a smile touches at the corner of her mouth. 'You shouldn't be concerned with what it is like to die. You should be concerned with what it is like to be dead. Dying is an instant. One moment you are living and the next you're not. What comes after is the stuff that should keep you up at night. I can tell you exactly what will happen to you if you want. Would you like that?'

I nod for her to continue and the smile widens on her face as she takes pleasure in the telling. The image of my own bloody entrails is fixed in my head.

'The problem with killing people is that they wait for you. They have nothing but time to plan for the day you die. There are many hands waiting to rip you apart, Aaron. They will pull you into a giant mouth that will swallow you into an abyss from which there is no escape. Your greatest sin will be nothing in comparison to the torment you will suffer. Your bones will break, your skin will peel, your eyes will be gouged ...'

I chuckle and it breaks Jane out of her stride.

'Please. You think that scares me? I've already taken the bus four times today. If there are people waiting for me after death then they are the ones who should be scared. If they have any sense, they'll leave me alone. Eternity is a very long time to be stuck with the likes of me. It's a shame to hear that people on the other side are as boring and predictable in death as they were in life. This afterlife business continues to disappoint me with every passing second.'

Jane's intensity deflates as her threat misses its mark.

'You're a fool,' she says.

'A living one,' I counter.

'A sad one,' she corrects. 'I pity you. Not only do you have to rape me to lose your virginity, but you also had to murder me first. You really are pathetic. Look at you. Why would anyone want to touch you? You're the most hideous thing I've ever seen. I only ever looked you in the eyes so I could confirm that a man as disgusting as you actually exists in this world. I would spit on you if I had the saliva.'

She hits the mark this time. I sit on the bed with wide, furious eyes and flared nostrils. My nails dig in and scrape at my naked knees.

'There it is,' I say through clenched teeth. 'You're just like the rest of the whores.'

'Whores that will fuck anyone but you.'

I take a deep breath to compose myself and count backwards from ten. It works, barely. It's a shame that I've already killed the bitch.

'I know what you're trying to do, but making me mad won't stop what has to happen here. By fucking you, I fuck you all. Anything you say will just make me enjoy it even more.'

She shakes her head and stares a hole into the floor, thinking of what might have been. Thinking of all the doors that I have closed on her.

'You really have no concern for anyone, do you? It is more than just my life you are playing around with. Have you thought of that? Your family is gone and soon you'll be in prison, with no one to visit you. Do you even have an ounce of regret? What about my boyfriend, Mark? I'll be dead and he'll blame himself, when he should be blaming you. Everyone should be blaming you.'

I laugh hysterically. This girl kills me, she really does. I even have to hold my ribs when the laughter starts to hurt my sides.

'What are you laughing at?' she demands.

'In all of this mess, you're worried about what Mr. Average is going to think? We both know that he is fucking someone else behind your back.'

'Stop it!'

'I've read your messages and I've heard you on the phone. He didn't come home to save you from me, because his dick was somewhere else. Most likely balls-deep in his ex-girlfriend, who he now happens to spend all of his time with. Of course he's going to blame himself. He should. He probably has her tits pressed up against some blueprints on the office wall as we speak.'

'No, he wouldn't do that. He's a good man, unlike you. You know nothing about him.'

'I know enough. There is no such thing as good. Only the things that we are willing to live with and the subjectivity of others. He's fucking her. Trust me.'

She is wringing her hands, pacing, shaking her head. I am playing with her fear and loving it.

'No, it would never happen,' but her voice is wavering as she says the words. She has thought about this more than she cares to admit. Time to go in for the kill.

'Oh yeah? Well, you don't have a body to tie you down any more – how about you just poof over there and see what he is up to right now.'

'"Poof" over there?'

'Yeah, poof over there. You can do that, can't you? Or are you scared of what you might see?'

'I'm not scared of anything, because he's not cheating on me.'

'Then won't it be satisfying to see the look on my face when you prove me wrong?'

She eyes me warily, looking for a deception.

'Fine. I will go have a look, but it's only because I want to see him, and not because I'm spying on him.'

'I think we are past the point where justifications are necessary.'

She seems satisfied at that.

'Don't you dare touch what used to be me while I'm gone. I'll know.'

'Wouldn't dream of it. This night keeps getting more and more interesting. I want to see how all of this plays out. Besides, I kind of want you here when I do the deed.'

Her face registers her revulsion at the thought, and with a 'poof' she is gone to some place to check up on Mr. Average. I turn to her corpse to help pass the time while I wait.

'Why can't she be more like you, eh? Not a care in the world.'

A moment later she's back, a single ghost tear running down her ghost cheek.

'Well?' I ask.

'I don't want to talk about it!'

CHAPTER EIGHTEEN

Jane's hands are white-knuckled balls as she paces back and forth in front of me. Her slender neck disappears into her collarbone as she hunches her stress up with her shoulders and carries it there.

'Holy shit. He actually was fucking her, wasn't he!? I was just taking a shot in the dark to fuck with you, but this exceeds my wildest expectations. Am I good or what?'

'I said that I don't want to talk about it!'

A whole bookcase comes crashing down in a fit of rage and breaks apart into planks. A tsunami of literature splashes across the floor. For a writer, she really seems to hate books.

'Oh no, you don't get away with this one. I need details. This is just too delicious to let pass. Was it missionary? Doggy? Was she riding him like a cowgirl? Was he spanking her ass? Did she call out his name? "Average, Average, fuck me Average!"'

She slumps down to the floor and places her head in her trembling hands.

'I can't believe he's cheating on me.'

'Don't act the fool. You suspected that something was going on, or else you never would have gone there in the first place.'

'I thought that was just me being crazy. I never actually thought that they were doing anything.'

'Yet there they were, making the beast with two backs.'

'I'm such an idiot. They weren't even at the office. I had to check over at her place. I know you're laughing inside that head of yours, because you're an asshole. Stupid Jane who doesn't suspect a thing. It's a great big laugh. You murdered me and now you get to laugh at me. I want to return the last twenty-four hours like an unwanted gift and buy a better day. This one does not suit me and it's the last day I'll ever have, thanks to you.'

'Is that what you really want? Twenty-four hours ago you were ignorant and, in your own words, stupid. Hard truth is all there is, whether we choose to see it or not. There can be no lasting happiness without making your peace with it. Your eyes are open now and to willingly shut them again would make you an even bigger joke.'

She scoffs.

'Is that what you are? Happy? How is hard truth treating you?'

'I'm not unhappy. I'm not really anything. When I look inside there is nothing there besides anger, but that's not a cause for sadness. I live with my anger all the time. I've grown to love it, in fact. There's an energy that comes with anger, that comes with no other emotion. Someone gets under my skin and suddenly everything is crystal clear. Anger gives me purpose and points me in a direction. Nothing gets me from one day to the next like anger. You should embrace the truth and all of the anger that comes with it, Jane. It's not happiness, but it's something more useful.'

Her eyes narrow onto me with a furious disbelief.

'You don't think I have anger? I have lots, but most of it is for you. You are my purpose here and my direction.'

'I would have said the exact same thing about you,' I say as I stroke her dead leg. She is not impressed by that notion. It would have been so much easier if she had just loved me. I wouldn't have to be so cruel to her. I could have shown her my gentle side. It's in here somewhere. I swear.

'What did you see in him anyway?' I ask. 'Look at you. You could have had any man that you wanted and you picked that asshole. What does he have that I don't?'

'A soul. A life without murder. Take your pick.'

'Funny, but I'm serious. What does he really have that no one else does? Because from where I'm standing, he's average in every sense of the term. I'm not much of a looker, but I am special.'

'Yeah. Sure.'

'I would have proven it to you, but that ship has sailed now. Do you think Mr. Average would kill for you like I have? All I have done today has been done for you. Are you not impressed? Is there not some part of you that is flattered that I went so far for you? That's special, Jane. It upsets me that you don't appreciate it.'

'Unbelievable. You're upset? This is what I get for coming back to argue with crazy, I guess. You can't kill your way to love, you fucking idiot. That's the problem with letting anger rule. It leaves no room for love and you die alone, like you deserve.'

My eye twitches slightly, but we're fine. It's all good. This is a good conversation we're having. Really helps clear the air.

'You can kill your way to anything. Death is by far a higher currency than money. When money fails, people die, and the ones that live get what they want. If you kill enough people then the whole world can be yours. Fortunately, I don't want the world – just you, Jane – and what I want from you is an answer. What is it? What did he have? Tell me that much, for all the death that has come today. Let me buy at least that much with my currency.'

She ponders the question seriously this time. It is probably a question that has been at the back of her own mind ever since she saw Mr. Average, red-faced with exertion, humping at his ex-girlfriend's fuck-hole. What did she really see in that piece of shit?

'He made me laugh,' she says finally. 'He had a great sense of humour about everything. That's something that you can't kill for.'

'You've got to be kidding me. There must be something else. That's an answer right out of some women's magazine fluff piece.'

'It's true. Even in my darkest moments he could make me laugh.'

A troubling memory bubbles to the surface of her face. She looks sad thinking about it, but still she smiles in spite of her sadness. A beautiful melancholy.

'I had an abortion once,' she says, and she lets the words hang in the air after she says them. They don't hang for long, because the words are heavy. They are an anchor she has been keeping inside of herself for quite some time.

'It was a long time ago and I was not the same then as I am now. I was young and not at all ready to start a family. I hadn't lived a life of my own yet. I had too many goals left to achieve before a family could even be considered. Mark was very understanding of my concerns and we decided that it was in our best interests to terminate the pregnancy and wait for a time when it felt right for us. We crossed the water over to England and had the procedure done. Even though it was my choice, it was still tough for me. I had always dreamed of being a mother and I felt like I had lost something of that dream. I was mourning for this child that never was a child. It was not a child because I could not allow it to be a child. Despite all of that, I couldn't stop thinking about what it would have been like to hold that child in my arms and nurse it from my breast.

'After the procedure, we got on the boat back to Dublin, and I didn't speak for days. There was nothing I could say that would express what I was feeling, so I didn't say anything at all. Mark took off work and he stayed with me through everything. He held me when I cried, told me stories to fill the silences and made me many cups of tea. He was amazing, and all that I could have asked for. He eventually brought me out of it by making me laugh in moments where I thought that laughter would never be possible again. He made me laugh until I forgot I was sad for just a moment, but that moment was enough. I knew that I could be happy again, and knowing that made me happy.

'I always imagined that he would be there by my side to make me happy. Making me laugh every time I felt sad. He gave me laughter, while all you can offer me is anger and death. That is what he had. That is what you'll never have. That is what I've lost.'

Her breathing is very deliberate as she finishes. Big, heaping gulps of air to fight off the urge to break down and cry. No tears, only oxygen.

'You're not laughing now,' I say. 'You're upset and he's the reason why. Do you still love him when the laughter stops?'

She is silent for a long time, lost in nostalgic memories from her relationship past. Each memory goes onto a scale and weighed as she searches for an answer.

'I don't know,' she finally answers. 'It's not a black-and-white question.'

'I bet that I can make you laugh.'

'You're not funny to me. You're pathetic. I look at you and all I feel is hatred and revulsion. I don't even know why I'm confiding any of this to you. You're probably getting off on it in some sick way, but you're the only living ear I've got left. How sad is that?'

'Just give me a chance. I know you're a tough crowd, but listen to this one. How do you make a dead baby float?'

She does not humour me with a 'how?' so I go ahead and finish.

'You take your foot off its head.'

There is no laughter.

'I tell you a story about my abortion and the effect it had on me and you decide to make a dead baby joke?'

'Yeah, it's relevant humour. Did you not like it?'

'Pigs,' she says. 'All of you. Pigs.'

'Who?' I ask.

'You. Mark. Men. You're all pigs.'

'Hey, I'm not the one cheating on you. I'm a one-corpse man.'

'A cheater and a murderer. These are the standards for the modern man. Let me take back everything I said about you being pigs.'

'You can go on thinking that if you like, but it gets you nothing. Labels and words don't change anything. You're still just as dead and still just as cheated on.'

'That's where you're wrong. It empowers me to name and shame you. To see you all stripped of your pretence and shown as you really are. You were right when you said I was ignorant and stupid, but now I see everything clearly. You've done all you can to me and I am free from your bullshit now.'

I smile down at her corpse and all of its promise.

'Men haven't done everything to you yet.'

She glares at me and the glare sends a vibration through the room. I shudder and have the distinct sensation of someone walking over my future grave, but no books fly to hit me in the face. Yet.

'I get it,' I tell her. 'You have a vagina and you want control over it. Fuck the patriarchy and all that jazz. I get it. I really do. Men have murdered you. Men have cheated on you. Men are to blame for everything that ever happened to you. But let us cut to the heart of this sentiment, shall we? It's never been about equality, it has always been about fear. Fear of men. You paint us all with your brush of fear until we are all the same in your eyes. Read enough of those blogs you and your kind write and you'll start to believe that every man is a potential something. Any man you date is a potential cheater. Any man walking behind you on a dark street is a potential rapist. The man coaching your kid's football team is a potential paedophile, and men are, above all, potential killers. We are so full of potential in the eyes of women, but it is all a potential to create fear.'

'Are we really doing this?' she asks. 'Are we really debating this while you stand naked over my corpse? You know, the one that you murdered and are about to rape. Just look around you. I don't need to make any argument because you are the living proof.'

'I didn't say that it wasn't true. I'm everything that you have ever written about. Your every worst fear realised. I am a man unrestrained. Violent misogyny made flesh. Your words and your self-empowerment are nothing to me. Though I wouldn't call myself a rapist yet. Your corpse hasn't said no.'

'I'm saying no! I am!' she paces and shakes her head in a fury. 'Do you even know what it is like to be a woman? Do you have any empathy for my situation at all? If you could put yourself in my shoes then you wouldn't do what you are about to do. Find that one shred of decency inside you and stop this. It's too much.'

I sneer at the idea and shoot back with venom.

'Too much? I say it's not enough. Empathy is not a factor here. I want more and you can't stop me from having it. That is all that there is to it. Your boyfriend fucked someone else and I'm going to fuck you. The world is full of people getting fucked without empathy.'

I wave my hand around the bedroom and the situation.

'This. I fucking own this. I made this happen when you told me it couldn't. You women dress up with your tits out and your legs on display knowing what it does to us, and you want to claim that you did that for yourself and not because you wanted every man in the room eyeing you up? Fuck that. And you wonder why the male gender is so fucked up. You fucked it up! You did! You want to know why we are in charge? It's because it's the perk we get for having to put up with your shit. We have the power because you can't stop us having it. Power is for those who take it, not for those who ask for it. If you tried to take it, we'd kill you. They say if women ruled the world then there would be no wars, and that is the biggest lie ever told. There would be a war alright, because we would pull you out of your nice, fancy offices and put you back in chains. We would rape you over and over again until you knew the true meaning of dominance and why we have it. Those that don't get with the program get put in the ground. Right now women have it better than they have ever had it, because we have allowed it. But there comes a point when you're just pushing your luck, and when you pass that point, that is when the men will start digging holes. There will be no empathy on that day, just men like me and women with nowhere to hide.'

I finish, out of breath, and notice that my cock is huge and throbbing. It's a power boner if I ever did see one. Jane sighs with frustration and shakes her head at a hopeless cause.

'You are obviously a complete psychopath with no hope of redemption. I feel sorry for you. You're not even capable of the most basic level of respect for your fellow man, so of course respect for women is going to be an alien concept to your misogynist mind. You're right, I can't stop you. But does this use of power make you feel good about yourself? Has it improved your life in any way? Because right now you look like a miserable piece of shit.'

The front doorbell echoes throughout the house before I can answer, bringing the argument to a premature close. My eyes widen to the size of dinner plates as Jane smiles.

'You're not looking so powerful now, Mr Man.'

CHAPTER NINETEEN

A doorbell rings, but everyone I know is dead. Quite the mystery. I run through the possibilities in my mind. I know that Mr. Average is fucking his ex, so it couldn't possibly be him unless he poofed over here much like Jane did. It could be the police, I suppose. I did leave quite a trail behind me, but I thought that I would have more time than this. The evening at the very least. Who could it possibly be? Think, Aaron, think!

'What's the matter, Aaron? Are you afraid? All that power and you still scare like a little boy.'

'I'm only afraid of things left unfinished. I'll finish with you, don't you worry about that.'

I wait a moment to see if the person at the door goes away of their own accord, but the bell rings again, this time more insistent than the last. Where did I leave my phone? I grab my pants and rifle through the pockets until I find it. The screen shows numerous missed calls from Frank Walters. The phone starts to ring again as I hold it in my hand.

'Shit. It's my boss.'

'Makes sense,' Jane says nonchalantly.

'What do you mean, "It makes sense"?'

'I looked him up and gave him a call, to tell him how unprofessional and scary you were. I hope you don't mind,' she says, but she definitely hopes the opposite.

This time the bell rings and keeps ringing, as Frank leaves his finger pressed on the button. He presses the bell with one hand and thumps on the door with the other.

'I know someone's in there!' he shouts through the letter box. 'I can see the lights on!'

I shake my head in resignation and start to dress. It's an unfortunate, mood-killing turn of events.

'What are you planning?' asks Jane, suspicious.

'Don't know yet. I'm not really the pre-meditated sort. I tend to just see what happens and deal with what comes after. It's an approach that has worked for me so far.'

The door thumps.

'Aaron!' Frank shouts.

'Yeah, yeah – coming, you old fart.'

I finish dressing as quickly as I can, before running downstairs towards the ringing, the thumping, and the shouting. I say 'Hi' to my mother. I say 'Hi' to my sister, and step out into the hallway, where I can see Frank Walters' angry silhouette through the frosted glass of the front door. I look back at the scene in the kitchen. Jane's ghost stands with a scowl, watching me closely. I shut the door on her judging eyes and the chaos I have created, putting them all out of sight and out of mind. I take a moment to compose myself. I can do this. I'll just see what he wants and send him on his way, as quickly as possible. Easy.

With a plan of action in place, I open the door and put an end to the incessant racket. Mr. Walters almost falls right through as his knocking fist falls ahead of him into the empty space. His moustache bristles with rage as he readjusts himself.

'Hey Frank. Is there something I can help …'

His pointed finger goes up to my nose and I back up a step.

'I had an interesting phone call today, when I should have been relaxing and enjoying a nice cup of tea with my wife. It's too late an hour for things to be interesting, Aaron. Do you want to take a guess as to who this phone call was from?'

'Um, a customer?'

'That's right, Aaron. A customer. If she stays a customer after what she told me you did it will be a goddamn miracle!'

'I don't know –'

'Don't you give me that dumb routine! I'm trying to run a business here!'

He wheezes out the word 'here', as he appears to run out of breath. He pounds his chest and sputters a cough, his face going a bright shade of red. It is the angriest I have ever seen him. The calm Frank Walters that I'm used to is nowhere to be found.

'Are you okay? You're not looking so good.'

'Bugger that! Bugger you! Bugger the doctors!'

He props a hand on the wall to steady himself and get his breath back.

'What do you have to say for yourself, hm?'

'I honestly have no idea what this is about, Mr. Walters. I'm guessing that a customer got a hold of your home phone number and told you some lies about me. Sounds like a crazy person if they went to all that trouble.'

'So, you're telling me that you didn't go through a customer's personal information and then harass them in their own home?'

I mime thinking, trying to recall the event in question, as if such a thing would ever need recalling.

'There was one lady who was quite odd. She called on the phone and said that she wouldn't make it before we shut for the night. She seemed to really need her laptop, so after talking for a bit I told her that I'd deliver it to her house before I went home. I did exactly that and when I got there she was very grateful, but then things got weird.'

'Weird how?'

'She was very clingy. She didn't want me to leave. Kept saying that her husband was away at work. I managed to get out of there eventually, but I think I might have upset her a little in the process. Is that the customer you are talking about? Jane, I think her name was.'

Mr. Walters calms his tits. His moustache is no longer bristling, but his face is still strained and red.

'Well, shoot. I guess that's that then. I'm sorry that I barged over here like this, but you weren't answering your damn phone!'

His face scrunches up in pain as he grips at his chest.

'Sure you're okay?'

'It'll pass. Just need to take one of the pills the doctor prescribed me.'

He takes a small pill bottle out of his inside coat pocket.

'If you don't mind, I'm going to get myself a glass of water.'

He moves to push open the kitchen door before I can stop him.

'No, wait!'

But it's too late.

'What the fuck!?'

'Yeah, I might have some explaining to do.'

'WHAT THE FUCK!?'

Mr. Walters doesn't walk into the kitchen, he shuffles, dragging his feet along the floor, almost unaware that he is even moving at all. In his mind, he's probably floating. His mouth hangs agape, taking in the scene that is in front of him. Two dead bodies, one at the table, one on the floor. He should run, but he doesn't. He doesn't do anything.

'I don't believe you've met my family, have you? This is my mother, and my sister, Rachel.'

'They're … dead.'

'You would think so, wouldn't you? But it turns out that the dead are not quite as dead as we first thought.'

'They're dead,' he says again with a little more conviction.

'I think you need to sit down. You're starting to repeat like a broken record.'

'They're dead.'

'That's right,' I say in a soothing tone as I gently guide him into a chair beside the dead body of my mother, which he has already observantly noticed.

'Sorry to put you to all this trouble, Mr. Walters. You said you were about to settle into some tea. Would you like a cup now?'

'They're dead,' he whispers, looking down at my sister on the floor. Still and motionless.

'Roast beef? We have plenty spare.'

'They're dead.'

'Just the tea then?'

I put the kettle on and throw a Lyons tea bag into a mug, as Mr. Walters' bottom lip starts to quiver.

'You like a lot of milk in yours if I remember correctly. One wonders how you even call it tea at all.'

When the tea is made I put it on a saucer plate. I open a pack of chocolate digestives and place a couple on the saucer beside the cup. I place the whole lot of it in front of the muttering Mr. Walters with a clink.

'There we are. Tea, just like you wanted. To help you forget about interesting things.'

He doesn't touch the tea. He just stares at it numbly and keeps on muttering the fact that he has already established.

'They're dead.'

'Yes. They are.'

His eyes become suddenly alert and lock onto mine.

'You killed them.'

'Yes. I did.'

His breathing starts to become panicked and erratic. He realises that he is prey sitting two feet away from a lion that has already caught his scent and bared its teeth. He pushes away from the table, knocking over his tea in the process.

'I have to go. I can't be here.'

I stand in front of the door, blocking off his exit.

'I can't let you go yet, Mr. Walters. We're not done talking things through. Sit back down, and I'll make you another cup of tea.'

He seizes me violently by the shirt, but his face is gradually changing from red to purple.

'I said that I have to go! Don't you understand?'

His grip involuntarily loosens as he staggers back and clutches at his arm.

'Oh, I understand just fine, but I don't think it's safe for you to go anywhere in your present condition.'

Mr. Walters sits back in his chair and struggles for the oxygen that would force the blood through his body. He reaches for his pills, but I quickly snatch them out of his hands. His pained grunt of frustration is the only response.

'What's even in these? Take too many of them and you'll develop a dependency. Before you know it you'll be taking pills just to take a shit in the morning. It's for your own good that I get rid of these.'

I pour the pills down the sink and he tries to stop me, but the attempt ends with him falling out of his chair and thumping hard against the floor, face to face with my sister. Their eyes meet and he somehow manages to scream, even in his present condition. His own mortality has never been so clear.

'You really are not looking well. Perhaps you did need those pills after all.'

I crouch down, just out of the reach of his desperate, outstretched hand.

'I guess this is where we say goodbye then. I've never talked someone to death before. Usually it's a far more violent affair, but I like it this way. Feels more civilised.'

The eyes are bulging out of his strained, purple face. Bloodshot vessels are clustering together to form two watery, red masses, where once there used to be white.

'Maybe you can tell me what it's like to die, as it's happening. A first-hand account in the moment would be interesting, don't you think? I am starting to understand death more and more as the night goes on, and it's all very fascinating. Tell me, what are you feeling right now?'

'Help … me.'

'It's too convenient for me not to. Consider it my resignation if you like. I get the feeling I won't be needing a job much longer, anyway.'

Spit flies from his mouth as he tries to pull himself up in one last desperate attempt to save himself. I watch him with detached curiosity as he falls again and starts to drag himself across the floor towards the exit. His whole face is covered in snot and saliva, hanging from his nose and jaw like bungee ropes. At last he makes it to the door, but finally stops moving. The prospect of opening it is one mountain too far.

I casually walk to his side and watch the life drain out of him. With his last breaths he turns to me and spits the snot and saliva with every word.

'I'll see you in hell.'

Perhaps he will, but he'll have to join the queue first.

CHAPTER TWENTY

There's no getting away from Jane. Her self-righteousness is an ever-persistent and annoying presence. She stands there with a sad face, judging me. Always judging. The recently departed obviously don't have anything fucking better to do than haunt the living. We are the reality TV that alleviates the boredom of death. I can feel her staring a hole right through me as I stand over the body of Frank Walters.

'What? Fucking what!?' I ask her.

'Why do you keep doing this?'

'I didn't do a thing. It's not my fault that his heart can't handle reality.'

'Stop this now. You need help.'

I point to the late Frank Walters.

'He needed help. You needed help. I don't need help. I am living the way I am supposed to be. Look at this poor sap. Spends all his life slowly building up a business, and for what? He's dead on my kitchen floor and it doesn't mean a goddamn thing. Are you going to reward him for that now that he's dead? I fucking doubt it.

'You wrote books. It will take a while, but those books will eventually go out of print and decay, until there is nothing left. Even the little girls who have read them will become old women and die. The only reason you are here now is because you're not happy with what comes after. I bet that the afterlife is a massive disappointment that couldn't possibly live up to the hype, and this shit show is all you have. And even this is fading away from you. There is no point to you either. Morality comes from people believing there is a point to everything and that they are special in this universe. They are not. It is all chaos and it means nothing. I don't need help, Jane, believe me. We should all be living like the world is about to end. What you call insanity, I call acceptance of the way things really are. That acceptance is what makes me different from the rest of you.'

'You always were a whiner,' says a voice that is not Jane's.

A new voice, but also an old one. I audibly groan as I turn to see the ghost version of my mother, standing there with her arms crossed and her foot tapping. By looking at her I can see that death does nothing to slim the figure. She looks as she did right before I stuck a fork in her eye.

'Hello, mother. So nice of you to join us. What's the matter – you couldn't fit through the pearly gates and they sent you back to do some jumping jacks first?'

She is shorter than me, but somehow makes herself bigger as she squares up to me with cold eyes.

'Your father says hello.'

That stops me dead. I whirl around the kitchen looking for any sign of him.

'Oh, don't worry. He's not here. He just told me to tell you that he's waiting. He's been waiting for a long time.'

I smile, relieved.

'Then he can wait a while longer. Why aren't you waiting with him?'

'Because I can't. I had to come and look you in the eyes. I needed to look in the eyes of a man that would murder his own flesh and blood. How does it feel, Aaron? You have no family now and you are all alone in the world. You have no one who cares about you. Not a soul to talk to. Tell me, son of mine, was all of this worth it?'

I look at the death that surrounds me. Death caused by my own hands. I look at it all and I smile.

'You're right. I am alone. That means I'm free. There's no one left to question me. I now live in a world where everything is right, even when it's wrong. How does it feel? It feels great now that you're gone. Those that would mourn for you are gone. Those that would judge me are gone. Once I've chopped your remains into tiny little pieces, I doubt that I or anyone else will ever spare a thought for you again. You won't even live on in memory. You struggled on after dad's death to provide for me and raise me, and for what? You're now dead by my hand. You are also pointless. Everything you have ever done has been pointless. This conversation we are having right now is pointless.'

The look on her face suggests that she is genuinely hurt by this notion. Even as I show her my true face, she still expects remorse, or some kind of acknowledgment. That her existence wasn't for nothing. That I feel something for her as my mother. She can go on expecting if she likes, but reality will never match up to the expectation.

'You always were an entitled little shit,' she says. 'All of this has never been about the futility of life, it's about how you get disappointed when things aren't handed to you. You never wanted to work for your reward but you always expected one all the same. Whenever a reward doesn't materialise, suddenly everything becomes pointless to you and life is cheap. You think you're different to the rest of us, but you're not. Lazy is what you are. We are dead because you're too lazy to fix your own problems and make something of yourself. I should have thrown myself down the stairs the moment I knew I was pregnant with you.'

A laugh escapes from me. I can't help it.

'There is a part of you that's my mother after all.'

'I'm your mother alright, and now I can say that being your mother is my greatest source of shame. But unlike you, I am not going to avoid responsibility. You are my son, whether you refuse to acknowledge it or not. Nothing will ever change that. I should have known what you were when you came out of me. You came into this world and you didn't cry, you didn't drop one single tear. You never cried at all. Every night you slept there was nothing but silence. I would stand over your crib and wait for my baby to need his mother, but you never stirred. I'm being honest when I say that you gave me the fucking creeps, but you were mine, so I loved you. I only ever wanted the best for you as your mother, but look at where that has gotten me. Has gotten us.'

My mother crosses the room and takes Jane's ghostly hands in her own.

'I am so sorry for what my son has done to you. You shouldn't have had to suffer for my failings as a parent.'

Jane shakes her head and pulls my mother into a hugging embrace.

'The failing is his. You don't have to apologise to me. It's all his fault.'

I roll my eyes at this bonding moment between the mutually dead. Next they'll be starting a support group.

'One of the perks of murdering people is that they are supposed to shut the fuck up when they die. Is that too much to ask?'

'Oh sorry, have we disappointed you, big brother?'

My ghost sister appears at my shoulder: poof. All of them dead less than twenty-four hours and they think they can 'poof' wherever they damn well please. They can all poof off.

'Not you too. I wonder if there's a good exorcist in town. The power of Christ compels you to all suck cocks in hell.'

Rachel ignores me and examines her body.

'Mum, look what he did to me.'

'I know, sweetie. "It all doesn't matter," apparently. "It's all pointless."'

'Can I hit him, mum?'

'Go ahead.'

'Hit me?' I ask, confused, but then the lights do their flicker thing and I am shut up by a flying toaster smashing me in the mouth.

'Jesus! Fuck!'

'Did that matter?' my sister teases. I glare at her in return.

'Get lost. All of you. Go towards the light or whatever it is that you do. I have something important that I need to finish upstairs and the novelty of your visit has quickly worn off.'

'No,' says my mother. 'We're not going anywhere. We're here to make what you did matter.'

I laugh, but the room is not amused.

'Good luck with that,' I tell them all as I start to walk up the stairs. No one follows me. I look down at the three dead women and they silently stare back. All of them are judging now. I can feel it in their gaze. It makes me glad that I killed them all. Fine, they can look all they want. It's all they have left and I will corrupt their vision by showing them things that they don't want to see. My mind turns to what waits for me in my bedroom. The beautiful body of Jane Flannery waits, in a starfish position on my bed. This Jane is asking for it and has no judgements. She has been waiting too long and is clamouring for the pleasure that only my love can provide.

This Jane has no interest in feminist debate, or hitting me with things. This Jane just wants it bad and won't complain one single bit as I go deeper and deeper into her lubricated and lifeless cunt. It is all that I want. The climax of all my hard work. My mother thinks I'm lazy? I'll show that bitch how wrong she is. My hand tremors with excitement as I reach for the door-knob. When I open the door, my room as I know it is gone. Instead it's my room as I knew it five years ago. The corpse of Jane Flannery is no longer present in the room and the three ghost women are there in its place. Their hands are joined together and their faces are the picture of concentration. The hallucination that surrounds me is clearly coming from them. Another cheap trick from the desperate dead.

'What's this now?' I ask of the room. 'Have you put me in a Charles Dickens novel? I suppose that you three are the ghosts of past, present, and future, or perhaps you can be the ghosts of fuck off, fuck you, and go the fuck away.'

The women remain silent and stand as a unit. Their eyes are fixed on a memory of me at the age of twenty-four. The memory sits slumped at the computer desk with the bright, blue glare from the open laptop illuminating his sullen face. The door stands open as the memory of my adolescent sister cartwheels out on the upstairs landing.

'Aaron, look,' she says after pulling off a sloppy cartwheel. The younger version of me ignores her and continues to absently look at the computer screen. He is hardly aware that she is there at all.

'Aaron. Hey, Aaron! Look! Look!'

Cartwheel after sloppy cartwheel he continues to ignore her, eyes only on the screen.

'Aaron, you're not looking!'

Finally, he turns and snaps at her pestering.

'What, Rachel! What is it!?'

Now she is startled and unsure of herself.

'Look,' she says timidly, as she executes another cartwheel, throwing in 'Ta-da!' jazz hands at the end.

'I'm not in the mood for this right now,' he says, before getting up to shut the door on her one-woman circus performance. He slumps back into his chair, upset. Rachel hesitantly opens the door a crack and sticks her tiny head through at the risk of getting it taken off.

'Is something wrong?'

'Just leave me alone, Rach.'

She comes into the room anyway and looks over younger Aaron's shoulder to see what is on the computer screen.

'Are you talking to a girl?' she puts a mock shocked hand over her open mouth. 'Is that your internet girlfriend?'

Young Aaron looks at her and silently regards his sister with wary eyes before answering.

'Not anymore. Turns out she already has a boyfriend and was never that into me to begin with. She just wanted the gifts I was sending her.'

'Really? This is what has you in a bad mood? She kind of looks like a whale anyway. Are you trying to find someone that looks like mum? Cause that's kind of weird, even for you. How would the sex even work? It would be like jumping on a bouncy castle. You'd be hitting your head off of the ceiling more than the headboard.'

Young Aaron laughs despite his bad mood. The laugh is genuine and not at all forced. He even shows a hint of some teeth in the resulting smile.

'That profile says she lives in Alaska,' my sister continues. 'Why would you want to go there? I bet they're all fruitcakes in Alaska because the cold freezes their brains and makes them go loopy. I'd say that her boyfriend is probably her cousin. The only people that live in Alaska are the ones that are already stuck there and can't leave. That leads to a lot of cousin fucking. I think you dodged a bullet on this one, bro.'

Young Aaron smiles after Rachel's successful attempt to cheer him up. She leans over and gives him a big, reassuring hug.

'Fuck her?' she asks.

'Fuck her,' he replies.

'Don't worry, Aaron. We'll find you a sexy bitch with big tits from a nicer climate.'

'Thanks, sis.'

'Now look!'

She cartwheels out of the room and young Aaron gives her a round of applause that she takes a graceful bow to.

'Is this the best you've got?' I ask back in the present day. 'You're wasting your time if it is. I don't give a shit about any of you.'

The room changes again, going backwards through time to my room of fifteen years ago. Objects shift and change to reflect the boy that I was then. I cringe at the sight of old band posters appearing on the wall. Nickelback and Creed smoulder at me. I am ashamed that my musical taste was ever so naive. The naive boy that I was is face down, crying onto a 'Stone Cold' Steve Austin bedspread. Dried blood crusts his face below the nose, and a swollen golf ball of flesh is raising itself above the right eye. He has clearly been through the wars, with the scars to prove it. There is a knock on the door and the voice of my mother from fifteen years ago travels through.

'Is everything okay in there? You ran upstairs without saying anything.'

She enters the room when she receives no answer and looks at her face-down son, whimpering into his pillow.

'Aaron, what's wrong?'

She goes to his side and turns his face towards hers. His eyes are red and puffy from the tears. Her eyes widen at the sight of the blood and swelling.

'Did something happen at school?' she asks.

'I hate them all! I wish they'd die!'

He turns his face away from her, ashamed to be seen in his present condition. His mother places a comforting hand on his back.

'Who did this? I'll speak with the Principal tomorrow.'

'I did this. I can't control things anymore and everyone hates me.'

'That's not true. I love you, Aaron, and I always will. I'm always here for you, you know that, don't you? Tell me what happened and I'll make sure it doesn't happen again.'

'No. I can't go back there. I can't go back to something I can't control. You can't make me, and if you do then something bad will happen. No one talks to me. No one looks at me. They just say things behind my back. I can't take it anymore.'

She is quiet while she thinks things over.

'Is this why you keep pretending to be sick lately?'

He doesn't respond and she nods to herself as if suddenly understanding everything.

'You don't have to go back there if you don't want to,' she says.

He turns back to face her again. His face is one of tear-soaked surprise.

'Do you mean it?' he asks through snotty sniffles.

'You're obviously not happy. Don't think that I haven't noticed. If leaving school will make you happy then I'll support your decision. You're my son.'

Young Aaron rises from the bed and hugs the memory of my mother tight.

'Thank you,' he says with genuine honesty.

'We'll figure something out, but don't you go thinking that this means you can sit around the house doing nothing. If you leave school then you are going to have to start earning your way. You'll look after your sister and you'll get a job when you're old enough. Is that okay with you, Aaron?'

He nods agreement into her gigantic bosom.

'I'll call them in the morning and tell them you won't be attending any-more. Now, how about we forget about all of this and I cook you up some bacon and eggs?'

He lifts his head and smiles at my hallucination mother. In the present day there are no smiles from me. They are the sole property of the past.

'Isn't this nice,' I say. 'It's like a highlight reel of minor kindnesses. Is it supposed to make me feel guilty? Is it supposed to change what's in my heart? It's far too late for these kinds of games and you all know it. The damage is done.'

The three dead women look exhausted, barely visible now. Their outlines are a faded projection, dying in the light of the room. They have expended a great amount of energy with their time-travelling movie show.

'I don't suppose you guys can get Netflix? No? Then how about we end this trip down memory lane so I can finish what I started. You've failed. Game over. You're nothing but a bunch of dead bitches that don't know when to quit.'

The lights go out momentarily and when they come back the room is as it is supposed to be. The corpse of Jane Flannery has returned to its starfish position atop my crumpled bedspread.

'You're all alone now, Aaron,' says my mother, taking a step towards me, her voice now hoarse.

'Excuse me?'

'All alone,' says my sister, taking a step towards me.

'All alone,' Jane repeats as she also steps forward. They are slowly surrounding me from all sides, forming a triangle of power.

'All alone,' they say in unison. 'All alone.'

'Shut up, all of you! I'm tired of this.'

'All alone.'

'I said shut up!'

I take a swing and my fist passes through my sister's head. I kick out and my foot goes into Jane's stomach and right out the other side. I headbutt my mother, but the contact doesn't even register. The air cracks with an electric energy that is concentrated solely around me. My possessions start to fly around the room, swirling in giant, looping circles, faster and faster. I stand in the eye of a tornado as the only living thing surrounded by the dead. The dead start to chant from their triangle formation.

'All alone. All alone. All alone.'

I can't take it anymore.

'STOP!!!'

The chanting ends. My books, my video games, my TV and more all crash to the floor, once again slaves to the natural order of things. The dead women are finally gone, their energy spent at last.

'That's more like it,' I say while struggling to catch my breath.

But it is quiet. Too quiet. I have that sinking feeling in my stomach. That feeling when your body knows something is coming but your brain is too slow to catch up. In the quiet I feel a faint rumble in the distance and that rumble grows into a sound. The sound moves towards me and as it gets closer, I can identify it as the sound of a car engine travelling at great speed. I hear the tires of that same car skid their rubber onto the gravel of my front driveway. The volume is returning, but now it is too loud. What I wouldn't give to truly be all alone.

147

A MOMENT FOR MARK KELLY

Our bodies were entwined, plugged at the crotch. I was close. Very close. The beginnings of a mind-shattering orgasm were running up and down the length of my cock. Rebecca wasn't as fit as Jane, but she fucked like a demon and that more than made up for it. The meat on her hips served as handles as I thrusted harder. I could hear my phone ringing, but my mind was somewhere else, teetering on the verge of ecstasy.

'Fuck. Shit. Just a little more …'

The ringing continued, ignorant of my near-satisfaction. It didn't know how close I was.

'It's her,' said Rebecca after a quick side-glance at the screen. 'You should answer it.'

I roared to the heavens in frustration as I pulled out of Rebecca. I really was very close.

'Don't you go anywhere,' I said as I picked up the phone. Jane's name vibrated on the screen. I took a moment to get my breathing under control and answered. Before I could even say hello, Jane was speaking. She sounded hysterical, rambling about some man called Aaron from the computer repair store she visited. I placed my head in my free hand and sighed. Jane had a habit of blowing things out of proportion.

'Jane … Jane … Calm down.'

Every time I tried to get a word in she would just speak over me so fast that I couldn't even hear the details of what she was trying to tell me. Rebecca gave me a coy smile from the comfort of the bed, her naked body a mural to hours of expert tattoo work. The woman was a literal work of art. I was eager to be back in her arms and to finish what I started. I could look at most works of art but so rarely did I ever get the chance to fuck them.

'I can't possibly come home,' I said when Jane finally exhausted herself. 'There's too much work to do. We have deadlines that need to be met.'

Rebecca knelt up on the bed and took my cock in her hands as Jane threatened to kick me out of the house if I didn't come home. Rebecca took me into her mouth and I didn't even notice that Jane had hung up on the call. I came and it felt like an earthquake with the way I shuddered. She swallowed every drop of it. Every single drop. Jane never swallowed. Jane never went south.

'Do you ever feel guilty?' Rebecca would ask later, as we shared a cigarette in bed.

'About Jane? All the time.'

'Then why keep doing this? Not that I'm complaining. Just curious.'

'You know why. I never got over you and you use that against me whenever you feel like it. Jane is this beautiful, wonderful person, but she never infatuated me the way that you do. Yet you want nothing more than what we have now. You toy with me and you love every second of it. One day you'll leave for good, but you won't sweep up the pieces of the things you've broken. You'll leave that for me and Jane to do. So yes, I do feel guilty. It breaks me up and that's the truth. I really don't want to hurt her.'

'You could always stop.'

'I don't want to be without you either. I want you for as long as I can have you.'

'You're a real piece of shit.'

'I know. You gonna fuck me again or what?'

She did. She fucked me so hard that I saw the dead. Jane standing at the end of the bed. One second there, the next gone.

'Get off me!'

'What?'

'Get the fuck off me!'

I had to physically lift Rebecca off of my cock.

'What the fuck is the matter with you!?' she demanded.

'You didn't see that!?'

'See what?'

I looked around the entirety of the room. I even looked behind the curtain just to make sure, but Jane was gone.

'Nothing … I didn't see anything. Listen, I have to go. There's some stuff I need to sort out at home.'

'What the hell is going on? One minute you're inside of me and the next you're bolting for the door.'

'I'll explain another time, but right now I have to go.'

I dressed as fast as I could and fled from the bedroom. An ornament smashed against the door as I closed it behind me. Rebecca was pissed, but in that moment I had a feeling that something had gone terribly wrong. I rang Jane's phone, but there was no answer.

'Come on. Pick up, pick up, pick up!'

I raced my car back home, ignoring all the speed limits, and barged into the house.

'Jane, are you home!?'

Again there was no answer. In the kitchen I found broken glass from a window that had been smashed in. I ran up the stairs, my heart beating hard in my chest. The sight of Roxy's broken corpse brought me to a stop. I shook my head and my lip involuntarily quivered, but no amount of head-shaking could undo what was already done.

I stepped over Roxy to find our bedroom empty with the light still on. Jane was nowhere to be found. She was trying to tell me something earlier, but I wouldn't listen. I was too caught up fucking Rebecca and something terrible happened because of it. I tried to recall precisely what it was that Jane was trying to tell me. She mentioned a name. Aaron. Aaron Walsh. He worked in a computer repair store. Yes, that was it. She was scared of him.

I found Jane's laptop on the bedroom dresser, the very same one that this Aaron had repaired earlier in the day. I searched the name Aaron Walsh anywhere that it could be searched and I got a hit. Better than that, I got an address.

I reached for my phone and saw several missed calls from Rebecca. The knot of creeping guilt tightened within my stomach as I swiped her name away and dialled 999.

'Hello, emergency services.'

I was already moving. I didn't know what was happening, but I knew that time could be of the essence.

'My girlfriend is missing and our house has been broken into. He killed our fucking dog!'

'Okay, sir, I need you to take a breath and tell me your girlfriend's name.'

'It's Jane. Jane Flannery. A man called Aaron Walsh took her. I'm going there now.'

I was struggling for breath and hyperventilating as I got back in my car. My emotions were starting to run away from me.

'Sir, I need you to stay where you are. I will send a car out if you have an address.'

'353 Collins Drive. Tell them to meet me there.'

'Sir …'

I hung up the phone. I didn't know if I could take being called 'sir' one more time. I floored it and my Audi R8 gave everything that it had. It was a matte black beast that roared through the city streets. I was going to find Jane and set things right. I didn't know how, I just hoped that it wasn't too late.

CHAPTER TWENTY-ONE

I move under the cover of darkness and creep quietly into my mother's room to check out the unexpected visitor from the vantage point of her window. The curtain is opened just a crack as I keep myself as invisible as possible. I think ninja thoughts and stick to the shadows. A matte-black Audi R8 is parked up beside Frank Walters' beat-up Toyota. I feel a case of stranger danger coming on as this car is not familiar to me. It is a danger from someone that has spent a little more than was reasonable on their mode of transportation. The Audi R8 parked in the driveway is probably worth more than half of the house I am standing in. It likely belongs to some small-dicked, arrogant prick who thinks they can just show up here in the middle of the night without any consequences. I have a way of dealing with arrogant pricks and you can probably guess what it is. They are nothing in the face of what I have already endured this night.

The doorbell rings and I make a mental note to disconnect that fucking thing at the nearest available opportunity. The whole point of having a door is so you can shut the outside world out. Why the fuck would you install something that lets you know when they want to come in?

'Hello?' someone calls through the letter box. It is a man's voice. A small-dicked man. I don't move a muscle. I don't even breathe. I watch and I wait.

The doorbell rings once more and I hear the crunching of footsteps on the garden stones. Small-dick backs up into my field of vision and looks up at the house with a concerned look on his face. I take a ninja step backwards just in case he can see me and then I take a good look of my own. I am more than a little surprised to see that the man in my driveway is Mr. Average.

'How the fuck?' I silently mouth to myself.

Mr. Average shakes his average head at the house and looks back towards his more than average car. Go on, I mentally urge. Go on back and fuck that stupid bitch you pulled out of to come here. It's not safe for you here.

I project all of my darkest energy in his direction, hoping that he will go away. Hoping that he will feel my knife at his throat, even if he doesn't see it.

Mr. Average takes a couple of steps back towards his car and stops. He is thinking. He is thinking too hard. He shakes his head once more and walks back towards the house. He skips the front door, opting to check the back entrance instead.

'Fuck.'

I continue to listen as he tries every door and window that he comes across.

'Are you there, Jane?' I ask into the darkness.

Her ghostly silhouette falls in beside me. She glows brightly in the absence of any other light.

'Do you know anything about this?'

'I might know something,' she says, but there is no joy in her tone.

'Well, it's no good keeping secrets now. He's already here.'

I can see reluctance etched across her face. She is deciding if speaking would be a betrayal. She is not quite sure what to make of the situation herself.

'When you told me to go check out what he was doing, I did exactly that … and I saw what I saw.'

She pauses, lost in the uncomfortable memory.

'Go on,' I urge, eager to see where this is going.

'He made eye contact with me. While they were doing what they were doing he made eye contact with me. I think he could see me. He was cheating on me, fucking her, and making eye contact with me. It was too much. I left before I could be absolutely sure he saw me, but I guess this proves that he did.'

'That doesn't explain how he is here now. How did he find me?'

'I told him all about you. He knows your name and where you work. It probably wasn't hard to find out the rest from there.'

I hear a window smash and I curse single-pane glass for more than just its lack of heat retention. Small dick he may have, but he's got big balls for coming here. He has gained entry into my home the exact same way I gained entry into his, but that is where the similarity ends. In his case it will be the last building that he ever enters.

'Don't kill him,' says Jane, as if reading my thoughts. Though it seems a struggle for her to get the words out.

'What do you care? He cheated on you. He looked you right in the eyes while he was fucking another woman. He's already betrayed you.'

'Doesn't mean that I want him dead. Please, I am asking you this one thing. Do at least this much for me if you do nothing else. Find a way to let him leave without killing him and you have my blessing to do whatever you want to my body. I'll even watch, if that's what you want.'

I see her sincerity and the possibilities run through my head, but I sigh those possibilities away a single breath later.

'It's too late. I have no choice.'

'Please. You asked me if I still love him. I do. I do love him. Please.'

'Why? Why do you love him still? Even now, knowing everything that you know.'

'I can't help it. Hurt doesn't make love go away.'

'Then I will send your love to join you in the afterlife. You can hurt together.'

I go back to silence. Back to listening. Back to waiting. Jane sobs beside me, knowing what has to come next. Knowing what she has to witness.

'Hello?' Mr. Average calls for the second time. This time as a trespasser.

'Jane?'

Jane stays by my side. Her feet do not move. Her body does not 'poof'. She stays exactly where she is.

'Don't you want to go to him?' I ask.

'I can't interfere,' she says.

'You've been interfering just fine until now.'

'I can't interfere in this. This is a matter for the living.'

I nod my understanding and smile.

'Good.'

I hear Mr. Average moving through the back rooms downstairs. Soon his path will take him into the kitchen.

'Oh my God!'

He arrives in the kitchen. There is silence now. Not even movement can be heard. My ears work overtime, more hyper-aware than they've ever been, but they hear nothing. I speculate on what he is doing now. The three bodies in the kitchen have likely confirmed his worst fears and frozen him with shock. He has two options now and the options are as primal as you can get. Fight or flight. If he opts for flight, he will be chased down and gutted like a pig. His insides will be used as confetti as I celebrate my superiority over all things average. Opting for fight would save me the hassle of having to chase him down.

'Jane!?' Mr. Average shouts more urgently than he had done before. 'Jane, are you here!?'

He takes a tentative step onto the stairs. The loud creak echoes throughout the house. I know that he is feeling the fear. How could he not? He has no idea what waits for him. I am the thing in the dark. I am the terrifying news headline that everyone thinks only happens to other people. I am every nightmare that he has ever had rolled into one and I am happening to him at this very moment. In spite of his fear he keeps moving forward like the brave fool that he is.

'If anyone is up there, you should come out now. You've been found out. It'll go much easier for you,' he says. They are confident words, but his voice betrays him. I almost laugh at his small-dicked arrogance and give away my position. But I am very, very patient. The laughter will come later when I add his corpse to the pile. The best laughs need a good punch line.

Creak, creak go the slow and steady steps of Mr. Average. I meditate to the rhythm, measuring the distance between us in my mind, preparing myself for the task at hand. The fool should have called the police. He thinks he can be a hero, when he is already too late. There is no princess for him to rescue. She is in another castle. He reaches the upstairs landing and pauses, unsure of himself. It's all too real now. I hear him moving for the only room that has a light turned on. My bedroom.

This time I have to physically swallow my laughter. It tries to escape out of my nose in sharp bursts of air, but I don't let it. It really is too funny. I will let him look. I will let him see. But I will not laugh. I must not laugh.

My bedroom door squeaks on its hinges and I get to my feet in the room opposite. I creep ever so quietly onto the landing so I can get a better view of this Kodak moment. I know all of the right places to step to avoid notice. I see his back in the doorway as he looks in. The sight turns him into a stone so solid that pigeons could rest on his shoulders and shit down his chest.

'Jane …' he says on an exhaled breath that he had been holding in. He goes to her, shaking her to make sure of what he already knows in his heart. He feels it: the coldness of her skin.

'No, no, no! Wake up, Jane! Come on now. You can't go on me like this!'

He doesn't hear me. He is too caught up in denial to notice anything else. The poor fool. He really should have called the police.

'There's so much that we need to talk –'

His words are cut off in a gargle as I come up behind him with a rear naked choke-hold that I learned from watching UFC. My forearm pulls tight against his throat. He struggles, but I have my grip cinched in tight. There is nowhere for him to go. He blindly elbows back in my direction, but I anticipate his every move and easily dodge the blows.

'It will all be over soon,' I whisper into his ear. 'Go to sleep.'

Desperately, he fumbles for his pocket as I feel him start to fade in my arms like a tired but stubborn child. He grips at something there and quickly brings it up in a flash of steel. I recoil as he deeply slices a sharp kitchen knife into the soft meat of my forearm, drawing a line of red. That's why the son of a bitch was so quiet in the kitchen! I stagger back with my arm cradled until I feel the wall behind me. Mr. Average sputters, and spits, and gets his bearings. Then he is on me; a shark that's got the scent of blood. His woman is dead and the man responsible is in his sights.

He lunges violently, with the knife-point aimed at my heart. I have just enough time to get my hands up and parry the thrust, but it is only parried as far as my shoulder. The blade sinks in deep and I let a scream escape into the night. The pain is hot and searing. He drives it in further, until there is nothing but the handle protruding. He twists, using the knife as a blender to make mince out of my shoulder. This is certainly not funny anymore. I pull my head back as far as it will go and I swing it forward to smash the bridge of his nose. Blood spurts in a crimson river, but he keeps hold of that knife. Twisting and twisting with that knife. I hit him with the headbutt again, and this time I smash against the top of his cheekbone. The impact reverberates back in my own head and I can feel the beginnings of a concussion as the room sings and emits a high pitched ring all around me. I ignore the shooting pain clusters in my head and swing with it one last time. It is a solid hit that finally backs him up, clutching at his bloodied face.

I reach to pull the knife out of me, but it is slick with my own blood. It takes some doing. When it is free, I raise it high in the air and stumble towards him, leaking more blood as I go. I plunge the knife in a swift motion, but he catches me firmly by the wrist. We struggle like this. I put all of my strength into pushing the knife down towards his face, ignoring the screaming protests of my shoulder. He successfully holds me off as my blood drips from the knife and falls like rain onto his face. I let myself get distracted by how picturesque it looks. It is enough of a distraction for Mr. Average to score with a bruising knee to the testicles. Air ceases to be a thing of this reality as I bend over like a choir boy, veins throbbing to burst out of my forehead. Mr. Average takes the knife away from me and brings his knee up again to smash against my downturned face. I spit blood and teeth on my fall to the floor.

I try to crawl away to safety, but my movements are getting slower by the minute. Crawling on my hands and knees, I resemble a geriatric turtle without its shell. But this geriatric turtle is still very much aware that there is a man carrying a sharp and pointy death, hovering over him like a vulture.

In my peripheral vision I see him make his move. He is on the verge of simply free falling with the knife pointed at my exposed back. It is time to make a move of my own or die. I desperately roll and kick a hard leg sweep at his ankles before he can fall down onto me. The move must have caught him by surprise, because it is more effective than I anticipated. It takes only a moment before his feet are where his head used to be, and his head on the wrong side of impact. He thumps to the floor, skull first, and the knife flies out of his hand, underneath the bed, and out of reach. He grips his throbbing head as I pay the concussion back. It gives me enough time to catch my breath. The contents of my stomach almost eject as I let my body have a moment to acknowledge the hurt that has been done to it.

I reach out for something to grab onto and my hand finds the leg of my computer desk. Slowly, I pull myself back to a standing position, right as Mr. Average also gets his sea legs. We lock eyes for a brief moment and then he is charging. He is charging and I am too weak to get out of the way. I am hit with a running tackle that lifts me straight off my feet and up into his arms. Mr. Average holds onto me tight like a teddy bear and just keeps on running until he runs me right out of my room and slams me hard against the landing wall. The plaster of the wall gives way against our combined weight and I fall into a dusty crater made within.

Mr. Average takes a step back and hits me with a left, right combination that spins my head this way, and then that. Skin rips where his knuckles smash me. My head is spinning and I start to get delirious from the blood loss. I look to the side as he takes another step back and I see that Mr. Average has three ghost cheerleaders. They love to see me hurt. Love to see me in pain. I think I say, 'Fucking bitches!' but in reality, it comes out more like 'Fuh buhch!'

Mr. Average runs his boot right into my face. Fucking bitches. Fucking bastard. My head goes right through the other side of the wall and into my mother's room. I help the wall with its destruction. I pound the opening wider with my fists and pull myself through the hole my body has made. I put the wall between myself and Mr. Average and fall into the comforting darkness, but I know that my reprieve will not last long. I sense that the end is near. I can't let myself give up so easily. Not to Mr. Average. Not when I got so close to having everything I ever wanted. I am more than him. More than average. More than everyone gives me credit for. I need to show him, her, show you all.

He enters the room and turns on the light to see me better. I am back on my feet, but swaying like a hula dancer after last orders. My fists are raised to fend him off, but I am too weak. He walks straight past my defences and slugs me in the face. The best I can do is to grab onto him to avoid a fall, forcing a close grapple. He tries to shake me off so he can resume his pummelling, but I hold on for dear life. I hug him with the enthusiasm of a long parted lover.

He pushes against my face, pushing me away from his chest. It is just the opening that I need. One of his fingers finds its way into my mouth and I bite down with full chomping force. Mr. Average screams as his hot blood gushes into my mouth, making the world taste of copper. I gnaw as he beats at me repeatedly with his other fist, but I don't let go. I cut through the flesh with my teeth and rip at the bone. I clamp down and wrench my head back until the entire finger comes loose with a sickening rip. The stump where it used to reside sprays like a fountain. Mr. Average does not stop screaming as he cradles his disfigured hand. I show a red toothed smile at my hard-earned advantage and wink at a shocked Jane Flannery, who is witness to it all. The only thought that crosses my mind is that it is my fucking turn!

I fuck his ear-hole with my finger and pull. The lobe rips right off of the ear along with the gauge tunnel. What is left behind dangles uselessly and looks like a chicken McNugget. In the words of Ronald McDonald – I'm lovin' it. He backs away from me, screaming. This is more than he ever bargained for when he thought he could play the hero. I run towards him as fast as I can manage and build up momentum before leaving my feet. I connect with Mr. Average feet first and land a solid, double drop-kick right out of a WWE wrestling show. The dropkick shoots him across the room and right into the window. A loud crack is heard on impact, but the glass somehow holds.

I don't let him off the hook. I let loose with a primal roar and charge, looking for the finishing blow, but the son of a bitch moves at the last second. The window finally shatters as I hit him with all of my weight. My body is moving too fast to stop myself from falling through. I reach out in desperation, trying to grab hold of something, anything that will stop me falling from a second-floor window. It is his wrist that I catch hold of. I catch it and it is yanked with all the force of my falling weight. It doesn't stop me, but it does take him with me. We both plummet from the second floor together. My father's face flashes before me, right before impact. I bounce hard onto my side and I feel both my left arm and one of my ribs break like twigs under a hiker's boot. My teeth clack together, with my tongue sandwiched in between. The resulting blood helps to drown the screams of pain into a foamy, red gargle.

I look over to Mr. Average, who is now looking quite below average. He is below average, but his chest still rises and falls despite my best efforts. With my good arm, I reach out and drag my injured body towards him. The broken rib makes every movement torture, even the simple act of breathing. I meet him in front of his fancy car. That nice and fancy Audi R8. It gives me an idea for the big finish. I rifle through his pocket and find the keys. It is almost like touching his dick when I take them in my hand. I am a giant, slippery, red worm as I change direction and pull myself towards his car. I sit up and try the handle, discovering that it is already open. The smooth, leather car seat is very inviting after the night's exertions. I let my body fall into it as I shut the door behind me. It's tempting to pass out sitting where I'm sitting, but there is still a piece of unfinished business on the ground ahead of me, and another back in the house.

I turn the key in the ignition and it gives a satisfying roar. I had always wanted to drive something like this when I was a kid, and now look at me. I didn't even have to work for it. I put the car in reverse and back up a few feet. It's an uneven line, but it will do for what I am intending. I bring it to a stop and let the engine hum as the headlights illuminate a bloody and beaten Mr. Average. He is still alive, still breathing, but that is something that will soon be remedied. I get ready to press my foot down on the accelerator, but I am given pause when Jane appears in the headlights. She shakes her head at me. Don't do this the head shake says. I nod my head back at her in response. It's happening.

Mr. Average raises a weary hand up towards Jane. Jane lowers her hand down towards his. Their eyes meet. He mouths the words 'I'm sorry'. It is a very touching moment that puts me in mind of the movie 'Ghost', only she is Patrick Swayze and he is Demi Moore. If this were a movie from their perspective then this is where the key part of the soundtrack would come sweeping in to perfect the moment and something would save them at the last minute. But this is not a movie, and this is my story. The only soundtrack is the roar of an Audi R8 engine and the song that I can't help but sing in my head. It just has to be 'Unchained Melody' by the Righteous Brothers.

I NEED YOUR LOVE

I floor it and the tires spit gravel.

GOD SPEED YOUR LOVE

I drive straight through Jane. She passes through my windshield and out through me. One tire falls in line with Mr. Average's head, while the other falls in line with his legs.

TOOOOOO MEEEEEEEEE!

There is a squelching sound as the left tire crushes his skull and pops out his brain like piñata candy. The car takes his life with ease, treating him like a minor speed bump. An average speed bump, if you will.

CHAPTER TWENTY-TWO

'Bastard!' Jane shouts as I get out of the car. She tries to hit me, but each blow passes right through with the sensation of cold, splashing water. She screams into the night and through the veil that divides us from death. It is a scream powerful enough to reach any with an ear to listen to its hurt and anguish. It travels and its pitch shatters the windows of the car that killed her boyfriend. Dogs bark in the distance and car alarms screech. The neighbourhood now knows that a banshee walks its streets.

Mr. Average remains dead beneath his own car and I almost slip on what is left of his brain. The residue on my foot looks like blood-soaked cheese curd. His position on the ground is curiously similar to that of my father's all those years ago. Jane falls to her knees in tears beside his ruined head. Even after everything she still mourns for him. I shake my head at her weakness in disgust.

'Gonna fuck you,' I say, but with my broken face it probably sounds more like, 'Gon fuh oo'

She doesn't even turn to look at me. She just stays on her knees crying over her unfaithful, dead boyfriend. I've broken her at last. She should be more appreciative. I did all of this for her, as much as I did it for myself. I am the one that has always been faithful to her.

I fidget for my house keys and stumble to the door, with my broken arm hanging limp by my side and my broken rib causing me to grimace with every agonising step. Opening a door with just one arm is harder than you would think, but I still manage it and force my way inside. It is a minor inconvenience on a most inconvenient night. My only thoughts are for what's upstairs. I pass the body of my mother without a glance. I step over the bodies of Frank Walters and my sister Rachel. I reach the stairs and have to drag myself up with the aid of the side rail. Each step is torture, but every one of them is one step closer to my reward. Life is pain while striving for pleasure, I tell myself. There is but one obstacle that remains on my path to pleasure, and it is an obstacle that stands in a lot of people's way. The obstacle of family.

They wait in my path now, sister and mother. They continue to defy me and refuse to go gently into that good night. Shoulder to shoulder they stand by my bedroom door, a union of feminine force glaring in my direction. I walk through flickering lights and into the face of a violent, indoor hurricane emanating from the family that used to be. The family that I murdered. The family that by all rights should stay fucking dead! I fight against the hurricane as picture frames and anything else not nailed down crashes against me. Every step I take is like walking up hill as the wind rises to match my resistance. It is a wind that is determined to throw me out to sea, but I will not be thrown. I refuse. As long as I have arms and legs with which to fight, then I will walk where I please and no woman will stop me. I am a man and it is my right. They know this in their deepest hearts. They sense my stubborn refusal and that my will is greater than theirs. I can see the source of the hurricane weakening and fading against my continued defiance. It is their last desperate attempt to save Jane's dignity and deny me what I have rightfully earned. I crest the top of the invisible hill and the wind is no more than a gentle breeze upon my face. I look my fading mother and sister in the eyes, triumphant in my victory. My mother says just one thing before she finally blinks out of existence.

'Don't.'

Then she is gone, with my sister, to wherever it is that dead things go when they are not bothering me. There are no more obstacles left. No more ghosts or people to stand in my way. They are all dead. Dead and gone. It has all come down to this moment.

'Aaron.'

It's Jane. She speaks to my back. Her mourning of people unworthy of tears seemingly at an end. Why is she here? She must know that all hope is lost.

'Look at me, Aaron.'

Her voice is gentle. Far more gentle than it should be. I reluctantly turn to face her. What words could she possibly say? What arguments could she have to sway me when nothing else has so far? I turn to face her and what I see roots me to the spot with dropped jaw. This is no dead woman that greets me. This is heaven personified.

Jane stands naked. Her flesh ripe, pink, and alive with her breasts and vulva bare for me and my eyes to feast upon. She is a renaissance painting in motion. The very air around her shines in a giant halo of light and radiates warmth. It invites me. It begs me to come. There is nothing in the universe but her in the centre of this radiant light. The vision smiles, and she looks me in the eyes. She looks me in the eyes and that is all that I need. I am her creature. I always have been, from the first moment.

'Come to me, Aaron. You have been waiting too long.'

I walk towards her pert breasts. I walk towards her perfectly groomed, moist sex. My eyes well up at the sight as I stretch out my one good hand to touch heaven. It is everything that I wanted and more. My hand almost closes around one of her breasts, but she steps back with a giggle, smiling at me coyly.

'Got to be faster than that,' she says.

I smile back and lunge out with my hand once more, faster than the last time. Again she evades me and smiles at her successful tease. My cock strains against the seam of my pants, ready to explode out of the fabric. It can't take any more of this teasing, can't take any more delays. My need is urgent, my appetite rabid. A twenty-nine-year case of blue balls, begging for release. I dive at her recklessly. I want her in my arms, my mouth suckling on her nipples, my fingers in her cunt, but she is not there. My happiness is an illusion.

I pass through her naked breasts, through her naked crotch, and I get shat out of her naked butt. It is not heaven that I see, but a downward staircase instead. My commitment is total and my feet have no purchase on anything but the air underneath. I hit fast and I hit hard, rolling from step to step. I have no time to process the damage of one blow before another is delivered to compound my suffering. I fall for an eternity and I play back all the wrong I have done, from my father's death to the present day. In the end, even I did not matter. My skull cracks and my neck breaks as I reach the bottom. It was a good run, but now it is at an end. Blue lights flash through the windows as the sound of sirens scores my death. They're in for a surprise when they walk through that door and find what I have left for them. I picture the shocked faces and the newspaper headlines. I picture the old ladies tutting at how far society has fallen. Aaron Walsh on the front page, a man who has finally made something of himself. It is my one last happy thought.

I see Jane standing over me. I see my mother. I see my sister. I even see Mr. Average and Mr. Walters and that stupid fucking dog. They are all looking down at me and smiling, but there is a knowing behind those smiles. A knowledge of the consequence that awaits in the life beyond death.

It is often said that you will be surrounded by those you have loved when you die, and perhaps that is true for the good and the just. My fate is to die surrounded by those who hate me, and those that I hate in return.

CHAPTER TWENTY-THREE

The sensation of death is a curious one. Picture a purple-faced toddler choking on a piece of food and a mother reaching in to remove the obstruction. I am the food and death is the hand that pulls me out. One minute I am dying and looking up at the smiling faces of hatred, and the next I am forcibly pulled up and looking their hate right in the eye. I look down at the corpse that used to be me. It is a lifeless, glassy-eyed and vacant thing. It is now nothing more than the meat-suit where I used to reside.

'That wasn't so bad,' I say to the gathered crowd of pitchfork holders. 'I don't know what all of you were complaining about.'

There is that knowing smile again. It's there on all of their faces.

'What?' I ask nervously, but then I hear it. The sound of leather cracking against leather. I would say that I went as white as a ghost, but that statement would be redundant in my present condition. I haven't heard the crack of that leather belt in many a year. The last time I heard it, it was in the hands of my father as he beat me with it. I look to the shadows and there he stands with the belt hanging down from the loop around his knuckles, looking every bit the man I remember from the day I shoved him from the ladder to his death. The family reunion is finally complete.

'So … How have you been?' I ask of him.

'Been waiting for you, boy.'

He stands stiff and rigid, his eyes not moving. His mouth a line broken only by speech.

'You should have stayed waiting. Don't you remember what happened the last time you used that belt on me?'

His head turns in slow motion. It is as if he has never used a neck before. He looks at the belt in his hand and seems confused by its presence.

'Oh,' he says. 'I won't be needing that.'

He drops the belt to the floor and takes a rigid step forward, like a man thawing from ice. I take a step back to counter and raise up my fists.

'At least I can't die twice.'

The old man stops and stiffly tilts his head, puzzled by the statement. Years of death has taken away his natural humanity.

'Death is only the beginning,' he says in a weary voice. 'Some things are much worse.'

His eyes turn red. You hear me? They turn fucking red. Two bright, piercing headlights, covering me in their hellish glow. He opens his mouth and shows rows upon rows of sharp, jagged teeth, moving back and forth like saws. The man is a walking horror movie.

'I'm not afraid of you,' I tell him. 'I am so much worse than what you could ever be.'

My father silently reaches out with his hands, but there is still a great distance between us. I take yet another step back as the crowd of the murdered watch in eager anticipation. There is a loud cracking sound as one of my father's fingers breaks of its own accord, twisting itself to an unnatural angle. The rest of the fingers follow suit one agonising crack at a time until my father's hands are mangled monstrosities.

'What the fuck is this shit!?'

The broken bones disappear, retracting back into his hand like they never existed in the first place. Loose flaps of finger skin dangle where his fingers used to be. I look at them in confusion as they start to grow. They grow long and wide, forming new muscles that give them a solid shape. They snake across the floor towards me as flesh-coloured tentacles. They continue to grow and get closer with every passing second. My eyes grow wide with horror.

'No! Stay away!'

They lunge for my voice and catch me before I can get away. They wrap around me like pythons and drag me towards my father, towards the red light that blazes in the depths of his eyes. If Jane was a vision of heaven, then my father is certainly a vision of hell.

'I'll fuck you, old man! You hear me!? When I meet the Devil I'll spit right in his eye and then I'll fuck you!'

As the tentacles pull me closer, his jaw unhinges and widens into a giant, gaping maw that leads into a dark pit. His mouth widens until it is as big as a door. I scream as I am pulled ever closer to the void with his red, dead eyes watching me from the door's peak.

'You think this scares me, but it doesn't! I'll climb out, you just watch. I'll climb out and I'll kill God himself! The motherfucker has it coming! I'll kill you all! Kill you …'

The finger tentacles slither up and penetrate into my mouth and nostrils, shutting me up. I gag and vomit as one tentacle travels down my throat. My eyes roll into the back of my head as another pushes through my nose and stabs into the soft tissue of my brain.

Hands reach out from the pit that is his mouth. Hundreds of them. Thousands. Numbers beyond counting. They have all been waiting along with my father for one such as me to arrive. The tentacles feed me to the hands and they pull me in every direction. My legs rip off at the crotch as another hand smashes my scrotum into juice. My cock is yanked away like a garden weed and my eyes gouged out with sharp nails. They pull at my head with fingers in the eye sockets, ears, nose and mouth. Their collective strength pulls it clean from the neck and stains their hands with blood. Jane approaches as my eyeless, severed head stays supported by the hands. She caresses my bloodied cheek and kisses my lips for the first time of her own accord.

'I hope it was worth it,' she says, before leaving me to my fate.

The hands savage everything that is left. They pull out my entrails and play pass the parcel. They make mince out of my heart. Everything I once held as my form is violently and systematically ripped apart, piece by piece, until there is nothing left but an arm supporting an outstretched hand, reaching out with all the rest. The mouth closes and there is darkness. There are no happy endings. We all die. We all suffer. We are all alone. All alone.

A FINAL MOMENT

There you are. Are you satisfied, dear reader? I am dead. Is that worth the price of admission for you? If you have endured this long then that is surely the result you were hoping for. But perhaps I am mistaken. Perhaps you are a dirty, sick fuck, and you were cheering me on with your cock in hand, stroking to every page. Well, I hope I brought you to a sticky climax. I hope that these pages are so stuck together that you have no hope of ever turning this book into a second hand store.

I always thought that I was special in some way, but I'm not. I realise that now. My flaw is being human and that brings me down to your level no matter how much I deny it. I wanted to transcend and escape the limitations that come with being one of us, but that force seeking to stop me caught up in the end. There were brief moments on my last day when I felt truly free for the first time in my existence. We were never meant to be free. Mortality is the curse they give us to keep us in line. Life, death – it is all just one big pointless exercise in human control. We are cattle to be herded from one column to the next with as few questions as possible.

They think that by telling this story I will come to show remorse for the things that I have done. So they make me tell it again and again, living it like I am still there. I end like I began, by dying a thousand times a day. A never-ending replay of what they consider to be my worst moments. But like a priest once told me, to be absolved you have to first want forgiveness, and I want no such thing from the likes of those who made this world. Those that keep acting like they have a moral high-ground over humanity because they made us. Fuck that! God's a dick, Lucifer's a pussy and they fellate each other's cocks when they think no one is looking. We give over our power to them so we can excuse ourselves from being strong. Being strong is too much trouble for most, but I am a man who was made for trouble and I am not sorry.

I may not have remorse but what I do have is regret. I regret not getting to fuck Jane. After all that, I still didn't get to fuck her. She made things seem less pointless for a brief moment in time. That was worth everything to me, and was why I gave my life to risk it all. If I ever get out of this deep, dark hole they've put me in then I might find her and fuck her yet. We'll save that for the sequel. I've got nothing but time. I can wait.

You might be wondering what the afterlife is like, and all I can tell you is that living is worse. Here I suffer daily and never have a moment's peace, but at least in death they are honest about your suffering. Living is pretending that everything is okay and that makes it all the worse. I don't envy you.

That doesn't mean that I don't fantasise about going back. If I could go back, I would kill even more people. I would kill indiscriminately, taking the war-mongers and sex-traffickers as well as the queue-cutters and reality-TV-watchers. Everyone deserves to die. The trouble with humanity is that everyone thinks that they don't. They tell lies to themselves to justify existence. I'd kill them all. Every single last one. I'd be the Santa Claus of murder, stabbing my way through humanity one chimney at a time. When the last person is dead we will finally have peace and not a moment before. We will at last achieve that moral high-ground, through murder.

Most importantly, I would kill you, dear reader. Right now there is nothing I would love more than to reach out of these pages and dig my fingers into the soft flesh of your throat. Hold your breath for me and picture it. Me, squeezing the life out of you. Picture it, and think of everything you have done in your life from start to finish. Focus on the bad. Think about all the people you've fucked over. The evils that have been committed because of your actions and inactions. Picture all of that and ask yourself one question. Do you deserve to live? Answer that one question before you sit there in judgement of me. Because if you don't, I'll fucking kill you, and you'll be down here with me.

AFTERWORD

Every chapter in this book has been redrafted to make you feel as uncomfortable as possible. I felt that stepping into the mind of a violent misogynist like Aaron Walsh should not be allowed to be a comfortable experience.

The bulk of this text was written around the time of the Sandy Hook massacre in the United States. I believe the aftermath of that event greatly shaped the narrative of this story. I remember going onto social media and seeing such fear of the male gender in the various blogs and hashtagged posts. I started to see a perception of men that is always there, as an undercurrent in our society, but is only visible for a short time when emotions are high, such as after a tragedy. It is the perception that a man is a ticking time-bomb that could go off at any moment and take not only your life, but also your dignity. To half the population there is nothing more terrifying than a violent misogynist, and I saw something there that I felt worth exploring with the character of Aaron Walsh.

I have always been interested in exploring the darker elements of human nature and why we do the horrible things that we do. I find the best way to learn is to go deep into the subject matter that most people are afraid to talk about out loud. I don't need to create a monster to make my story a horror. I merely need to write a human being with all of the worst characteristics we are capable of. There is nothing more terrifying than the mirror we hold up to ourselves.

This book certainly took its toll on me on a personal level. There were nights when I'd wander the house openly weeping, not knowing the cause. There were other nights when the thought of gouging one of my own eyes out seemed an attractive proposition. When the book was finished, the crying stopped. The urge to gouge out my own eye stopped. This book brought me to the brink of insanity and then stopped. Everything just stopped, and I breathed a sigh of relief. I do like having my eyes.

I learned a great deal through the writing of this book, and I hope that you enjoyed it. If you did like what you saw, then I hope that you will leave me a favourable review on a website of your choosing. Reviews are hard to come by for fledgling authors such as myself. Be sure to keep up with all my latest news by visiting my website at michaelmcgovernblog.com and signing up to my social media at:

facebook.com/michaelmcgovernwriting
twitter.com/mikeymcgovern
instagram.com/miholik

Until next time,
Michael McGovern

ABOUT THE AUTHOR

Michael McGovern was born in Perth, Australia, to Irish parents. He relocated to Dublin, Ireland, at a young age and took a keen interest in writing. He dropped out of secondary school due to his fucked-up nature and became a pro wrestler for a while (true story). After he grew tired of wearing spandex, he bounced around from one customer service job to another until his hair fell out and he couldn't take it anymore. In secret he conspired to follow through on his dream to become a published writer. You can find him on the web at michaelmcgovernblog.com.

ACKNOWLEDGMENTS

I would like to thank my wonderful parents, Kieran and Carol McGovern. Over the years they have been nothing but supportive of me and I could not wish for a better home to have grown up in. I only have the luxury of doing something like this because of the stable home they have provided for me. I appreciate them more than they know.

A shout out to all my beta readers: Emmet Driver, Karl Fogarty, and Robert Hanly. Their invaluable feedback helped to shape the final draft of the book you now hold in your hands.

And finally, a big thank-you to the people at Carrowmore for all of the self-publishing services they provided to me, and to Mila at milagraphicartist.com for her excellent work on the cover.